I0659054

# Hearts in Danger

# SAGE ADVICE

# SANDRA CARMEL

Sage Advice
ISBN # 978-1-80250-774-4
©Copyright Sandra Carmel 2024
Cover Art by Kelly Martin ©Copyright June 2024
Interior text design by Claire Siemaszkiewicz
Totally Bound Publishing

Published in 2024 by Totally Bound Publishing, United Kingdom.

Totally Bound Publishing is an imprint of Totally Entwined Group Limited.

# SAGE ADVICE

# Dedication

For those who believe in second chances…
You, people and the universe are forever
evolving, and if we stick to initial impressions
and aren't open to change, we will miss out on
some incredible, life-enhancing opportunities.

# Chapter One

"Visit Alexander? No way. No. Way. He was an arrogant prick to me back in the day." Sage Cassidy shook her head, adamant, and refocused on her laptop screen. And yes, okay, she might still harbor some slight, unresolved feelings following his rejection.

"Prick? That's a bit harsh. I know he can be stand-offish." Chase stared at her with his over-observant lawyerly eyes. "Did he do something you didn't tell me about?"

Where did she start? She raised her eyebrows in a challenge her brother couldn't win. Chase had blind loyalty to his best mate. He couldn't refute her, unless he knew something she didn't.

Which was entirely possible, considering she hadn't communicated with, let alone seen Alexander Barrett in fifteen years. "You mean, other than him treating me like crap since I turned twelve — teasing or ignoring me, then essentially ordering me to fuck off when I tried to hang out with you guys?"

Chase sat forward and propped his forearms on his knees. "Okay, fine. I get that he can be gruff, but he has a good heart."

Ironically, Alexander's gruffness turned her on, the idea of trying to win his affections...except he'd looked at her like she represented some defective female alien from another planet.

Sadly not surprising given she'd been a gawky rather than pretty teenager. So, massive fail. Her crush's supposed *good heart* left long-lasting effects.

Not that he'd have any inkling about the impact he'd had on her love life, men, relationships. As a psychologist, working in the trauma field in Melbourne for years, she should really talk about her unresolved feelings in her supervision sessions but...avoidance continued to be her favorite coping—more accurately, *non-coping*—strategy. "I can't see him. Sorry."

"Sis, please...for me. He's had a really rough time. He can't return to the military, and he's feeling lost, useless, helpless, when he's used to fighting for his country. Being the tough guy. Invincible." Chase focused his imploring eyes on her, his fingers fiddling with his platinum and sapphire cufflinks, the ones their now-deceased parents had given him as a graduation present.

How could she say no to that? She knew all about military-induced post-traumatic stress disorder. She'd specialized in it, worked with ex-service staff every day using eye movement desensitization and reprocessing—EMDR—therapy, combined with counseling. It constituted her bread and consistently warm, melting butter...when her intervention worked. And it didn't always.

"Did you explain you'd be asking *me* to make contact?"

"Yeah." He tugged at the sleeves of his expensive, immaculately pressed navy suit. Between that and the crisp white shirt, he looked fresh, like he'd just gotten dressed. He hadn't, though. He'd been in court all morning. 'Workaholic' had become his middle name — dependable brother, workaholic, best friend.

"And he was fine with it?" She couldn't believe Alexander had agreed.

"Totally. He refuses to speak to a stranger. He even refused to talk to me!" Chase slammed his hand to his chest. "That's when I realized things were serious. I tried to get him to open up for hours and…nothing. He said he didn't want to burden me, that what he'd seen had changed him permanently and the one steady thing was our friendship — something he didn't want to jeopardize. I get that. Well, maybe not 'get it' exactly, but I can empathize."

Chase adjusted his paisley tie. She'd never seen her brother so rattled. Normally he radiated confidence bordering on cockiness.

Sage nodded. She sensed he still had more to offload, more to say to attempt to get her onboard. And he excelled at arguing, debating.

"I convinced him to speak to someone, and he agreed, under one condition. It had to be a person he felt comfortable with, but no one too close. I thought of you straight away. Plus, given your specialty…"

Disappointment stabbed at her heart. *Bloody, unresolved emotional crap.* It wasn't like Alexander had ever shown a hint of interest in her romantically, even though she'd wished he'd finally *see* her — the *real* her, her as a grown, self-assured, desirable woman, not Chase's awkward, bothersome sister.

Instead, he'd demonstrated the exact opposite — except that one night when they nearly kissed, right before he left for the military...after his farewell bonfire. They were alone, and she ran her hand over his newly close-shaved hair, assuring him he looked cool, tough, mean, and no one would want to mess with him.

He'd grabbed her wrist, the flames of lust in his eyes practically melting her panties. Things suddenly shot to super-heated, scorching.

Until they didn't.

Like usual, he turned as frosty as a snowman in a blizzard and backed away.

For a split second, she could have sworn he'd been about to cross — no, obliterate — a boundary. It had to have been in her imagination. People often remembered past events in skewed, unrealistic, exaggerated ways, going by her dealings with clients and her own experience.

After the almost-kiss, she hadn't seen or spoken with him. Years had passed, and she had no idea how he looked, who he even was anymore. She should feel neutral, relaxed, confident seeing him.

She didn't.

If only rational thought overrode emotions.

Lingering feelings swirled around her heart. There had always been something about the infuriating man that sparked like kindling in her blood.

Sage swung her hair over her shoulder. Her resigned tell, according to her supervisor. "Fine. Give me his contact info, and I'll arrange to drop by. But just so you know, I can listen and refer him on, but I can't treat him. It goes against the Australian Psychological Society's Code of Ethics."

Her brother's grin stretched over his face. She almost expected him to fist-pump the air, like he did when he told her about a winning case. Chase grabbed his mobile out of his trouser pocket and started text messaging.

Sage's phone buzzed, Alexander's address and phone number flashing big and bold on the screen. "Received."

Her brother jumped up and wrapped her in a grateful hug. "You don't know how much this means to me."

"I think I do, and you owe me at least twelve months of wine and a selection of gourmet cheeses."

He pulled back, his facial expression shocked, incredulous. "What? Twelve months! You have to be kidding. That's milking it, big time. He's my best friend, but you know him, too. And you're a great person, a selfless person, who loves helping others, so —"

She raised her hand. "Stop right there." He forgot she was also well versed in his conflict-resolution, some might say guilt-inducing, coercion strategies. "Point taken. I'll settle for a case of wine with a mix of sparkling rosé, shiraz and fortified. "And a quarterly supply of Romano, gorgonzola and smoked goat's cheese." She would not compromise any further. Even if he did the 'cute-come-on-sis-puppy-eye-pleading' thing, something he'd mastered that usually won her over.

Chase's charming smile lifted the corners of his lips. It hadn't worked on her for ages — however, she could see how his Chris Hemsworth vibe and expertise at reading people could suck in the ladies. Men, too.

As a high-end solicitor, he used a more hardball rather than therapeutic approach. He had to play those involved, negotiate, have a solid poker face, know when to fight his battles and when to cut his losses.

He would have determined reasonably quickly that he'd pushed her as hard as he could. Push her too far and she'd retreat. "Got it." He saluted her. "I'll leave you to" — he waved his hands above her desk — "this."

Chase left her office, and she stared at Alexander's details on her mobile phone. She debated whether to call or text. Given her phone phobia and 'Alexander anxiety', she decided to text.

Normally she'd have her personal assistant follow up, but this was off the books...purely personal. Assisting an old friend... Well, a not-that-old, sexy, off-limits, totally unreciprocated friend of her brother's.

She sent Alexander an SMS, put her phone on the desk and, not even a minute later, it buzzed.

What now? Another unnerving message? Another veiled threat to her life? Something she'd almost thought she'd become desensitized to.

Until it happened again.

And again.

And again.

Working in the psychological trauma field, she expected angry, unhappy patients, but this one in particular liked to taunt. They hadn't hinted at any specific danger yet, so she'd let it go.

Sage had her suspicions about possible suspects, though hadn't taken action. Her clients were troubled, which was why they saw her in the first place. She didn't want to exacerbate their issues by possible false accusations. She didn't want them hassled prematurely by the police.

Otherwise they'd lose what little trust she'd been able to gain. And that would ruin the rest of their therapy, prevent them from ever moving forward positively, putting their faith in another professional, taking the risk on another psychologist, taking a risk on themselves and their decision-making.

She swiped her mobile screen. Like she didn't already have enough on her more-than-full plate.

Alexander. Relief flooded her veins while her heart thudded like a gong in her chest.

*Sage, hi. Long time no communicado. Thanks for making contact. I wasn't sure you would. When are you free? I'm at your disposal.*

Her breath hitched. Why did that sound so sexy? Almost flirty. He obviously hadn't meant it how she'd read it. She had to keep her response clear, simple, to the point. No ambiguity.

*Tonight at around 6 p.m. or tomorrow mid-morning.*

*Tonight. Please. My address is…*

Tonight? She'd thought it'd be too short notice. She'd expected to have more time to get herself together…her feelings, her readiness. Maybe Chase was right. Maybe Alexander's situation needed more attention than either of them had anticipated.

*Fine. See you soon.*

Images of him popped into her mind. As a nineteen-year-old he'd been tall and lean and strapping…a true fitness fanatic. And those eyes… She could never forget their deep blue intensity, like a lagoon in paradise. His gaze alone had her fighting an inevitable blush.

Thankfully, her olive skin had helped hide her reaction. If he'd realized she'd had such an all-encompassing crush on him, she'd have been mortified.

But now, with his years of experience in the world, would he notice? If not through her skin tone, through her body language? See through the subtleties of her highly developed mask, her measured responses?

And how about him? Would the clichéd windows to his soul show his pain? Would he have that lost stare in his eyes? The one she'd seen so many times — a mixture of grief, loss, despair…helplessness.

Reintegrating ex-service men and women into civilian life posed a significant challenge. Their bodies and brains had become addicted to the adrenaline rush, the anxiety of combat, and struggled to cope with the mundane every day, how they fit into society.

From what her brother had said, Alexander seemed affected by the usual PTSD symptoms — unrelenting nightmares, persistent flashbacks, disassociation from reality. She prided herself on providing sessions that explained the phenomenon in a caring, sensitive way and engaging clients in effective, evidence-based treatment.

Sage couldn't get involved with Alexander, though — not personally, not professionally. She'd have to give him impartial advice and refer him to a service that could objectively explore his situation in more depth.

From her interventions with clients, she'd learned they often required a healthy reset, some time to readjust. It reinforced that soldiers needed a therapist who wasn't conflicted and space to readapt, a skill they knew well.

Having chatted with a range of veterans, she understood that in a war zone they quickly and efficiently reacted in order to save others' lives in addition to their own. Could she help Alexander, too?

At least put him on the right path without getting too entangled?

Positive change could take its toll. It wasn't enough for some veterans to be out of immediate danger. Many times her clients experienced recurring night terrors that brought them right back to the scariest, most guilt-and-remorse-ridden situations of their lives.

And it felt real, almost tangible. They described the explosive sounds, the smoky smell, the metallic taste. A high percentage of her patients relived it daily. Forget all the other complications. It fucked with a person's psyche, their state of mind, their self-worth. Everyone needed time to reacclimatize.

In her case, with Alexander, she didn't have as much preparation time as she'd prefer. And she had no idea how long she'd need. Most likely she'd never be entirely ready. Given their text-exchange agreement, she only had a few short hours to psych herself up.

Would he continue to see her as Chase's annoying little sister? An irritating, yet possibly helpful hassle he had to deal with on top of his emotional, mental and probable physical scarring? Or would he take her suggestions onboard, her advice, acknowledging her professional expertise?

Did it even matter? She'd do her best and hope he got something out of their informal chat. Then, if he found it useful, she'd suggest a referral to an external, unbiased professional. Knowing him, even a little, could cause a competing interest. Her damn irrational emotions had already been triggered.

The best advice came from an unprejudiced place, hence why he needed someone independent, someone unbiased to provide intervention in the longer term. If she got him to understand that, she'd consider the interaction successful. Professionally, anyway.

Sage leaned into her office chair, closed her eyes and blew out a long, centering breath. She could do this. Like her brother said, she loved helping. So why should Alexander be any different?

Because he always would be, had always been special. Branded himself on her soul…irreplaceable, irremovable, permanent.

A familiar ding announced she had a new email. She snapped her eyes open and —

*Not again.* Goosebumps prickled along her skin.

Her heart galloped and her mind went AWOL.

The message frequency continued to escalate — sometimes email, sometimes text, sometimes social media. *Not a good sign.*

No. She shouldn't jump to fear-based conclusions.

Not yet. Before she went to the police, she needed more concrete evidence to prove she was in jeopardy or else they'd laugh her out of the station.

Getting a reputation as a jumpy, neurotic, hypersensitive psychologist wouldn't help her business.

The newest unsettling message sat at the top of her inbox and practically glared at her. The same email address as all the others. Some generic thing that undoubtedly couldn't be traced.

The title drew her eyes to it like a magnet.

*Time is running out…*

Curiosity got the better of her over-vigilant mind, and she clicked into the body of the email.

*You'll soon get what you deserve.*

Dread burned her stomach as though she'd sculled a double shot of cyanide. Like the other posts, it wasn't an overt threat. It could be interpreted any number of ways. And she refused to play into this person's game. Whoever had instigated this attack obviously hoped it'd put her on edge, unnerve her, make her fearful. Fuck her up.

And yes, okay, it did. It had…somewhat. She tried not to be the last to leave the office, made sure daylight still hung in the sky, warily checked the car park and held her keys in her hand like a makeshift knuckle duster.

Sage knew all about the power of paranoia, had seen it countless times in her therapy sessions—how it insidiously took over her clients' lives. She wouldn't allow that to happen to her. Her profession should make her immune. Right? She understood how it worked.

Rather than block the sender, she moved the email into a separate 'Threats' folder in case she needed evidence later. She'd also kept all the text messages and private-messenger social-media posts as a backup.

Over the years she'd heard too many stories of disgruntled patients attacking their therapists. Hopefully it wouldn't get to that. However, it paid to be cautious.

# Chapter Two

Alexander rolled out of bed before midday — the first time he'd managed it since being forced to leave the commandos. That had to be a positive. *Yeah?*

He padded into the bathroom in his boxers. He'd always been a hot sleeper. Nothing had changed there...except the nightmares. Now he frequently awakened in a pool of sweat with lingering stress. Today was no different.

Though, these days, he lived in the safe civilian world and expected female company. No, not of the sexual-satisfaction variety, unfortunately. He could really do with a good fuck, a no-strings-attached session with no names and no emotional entanglements. Purely fun, a physical release.

In theory, it sounded like the perfect solution. But it had never truly hit the spot. He'd tried — and tried and tried. What would make a difference now?

*Sage.*

Her name popped into his head whenever he was tempted. In the last two years, he'd pushed past his short-term-gratification urges, unable to follow through. He hadn't been in the right place, his deep-seated emotional injuries, his previous lack of fulfillment preventing him from bringing a random woman into his bed.

And even if he had, what if he woke up to her fearful screams, him pinning her down in a daze, a knife to her throat?

*His* knife.

*His* hand.

Reliving past scary-as-fuck, seemingly real events.

He couldn't live with himself, so he'd resorted to hermit status. But Chase, his annoying, well-meaning best mate, had used his brilliant strategic words to convince him to seek help.

After a long, hot, rejuvenating shower, he threw on a fresh pair of boxers and a T-shirt, made some breakfast and logged into his laptop at the kitchen bench.

Once he'd completed the obligatory trawl through his emails and social media, he washed the dishes and moved to the couch, propping his computer on the coffee table. He should spend some time searching for work possibilities, but he didn't know where to start.

Could Sage exorcise his demons? Assist him to discover his new life direction? And would he still harbor unresolved feelings for her? Maybe they'd meet and it would all be different. Maybe it'd reinforce that he'd finally moved on.

Hopefully it wouldn't set him back. He'd be a fucking idiot if he refused help from a professional who specialized in treating trauma — even if she was the girl who haunted his dreams, the girl he could never forget.

He'd sworn to stay away from her for fear it would affect his friendship with Chase. And he didn't want to be the dodgy, creepy, older guy hitting on his best friend's younger sister.

So he'd played the I-don't-give-a-fuck card. But he fucking had. As soon as she'd turned sixteen, she'd gone from grating little sister to drop-dead sensual woman—a full-on horny guy's wet dream.

His anyway.

He'd tried not to rake his eyes over her, take in her sweetness, the softness of her skin, her pure, natural beauty and almost fucked that up before he departed.

Alexander closed his eyes and rested his head against the couch before a knock on the door roused him from a nap. Jetlag still plagued him, even though he'd been back a couple of weeks, probably complicated by his PTSD. He glanced at the time on his mobile phone.

*Fuck.* Six p.m. already. Where had his afternoon gone? He really needed to get into a routine. Racing into the bedroom, he pulled on some sweatpants and answered the door on the second knock.

*Sage.*

*Fuck me.* Her amber eyes pierced him with their potency. He had always appreciated her beauty but...*wow. Frickin' gorgeous. A stunner.*

Her long black dress and high-heeled sandals enhanced her trim figure and gave off a professional-yet-approachable vibe. She didn't wear too much make-up, either—just enough to take the shine off her skin and emphasize her enthralling, unusual eyes. Low maintenance yet sexy. Exactly what he liked.

"Hey, Alexander."

"Alex, please."

She glanced down as if almost embarrassed. "You've always been Alexander to me. It's just...that's how I see you, know you."

"Whatever you're comfortable with." And he meant that. He didn't want her stressed. In fact, his head and stomach pressurized with an almost crushing need to say sorry.

She met his gaze, the intensity almost flooring him. His emotions hadn't been this stirred up by the sight of a woman since that last night, before he moved away.

He'd wanted to kiss her so bad, his whole body thrummed with desire. Ached. The pressure built until he thought his balls, if not his brain, would explode. He'd leaned in, her arms twined around his neck, her beautiful, innocent body pressed against his and…he couldn't do it.

As though solidifying his decision, Chase had called his name. He couldn't be seen kissing the guy's sister. They'd jolted apart like they'd been caught. Thank fuck his best mate hadn't seemed to witness what had almost happened. It wouldn't have been fair to Sage, to him, to his friendship with Chase.

"Alexander?"

*Shit.* He'd zoned out, her heavenly voice yanking him from his nostalgic thoughts. He stepped back. "Come in, please."

He led her into his living area. "Drink?"

"I'd love one." Her intoxicating musk-rose scent wafted over him.

"Hot, cold, alcoholic?"

She sat on the two-seater lounge, a smile breaking out on her lips that reached her irresistible eyes. "A coffee would be great…if you have the good stuff. Otherwise, don't worry"

He chuckled. "Pods okay? I have a machine."

"Totally fine. A long black, please."

Same as him. She used to like milk and sugar. When had that changed? He'd missed so much, yet also gained a hell of a lot, too. Life had a way of balancing everything out—or at least he hoped it would.

Alexander made their coffees, while they engaged in small talk, slightly easing the sexual tension, and handed her a cup. He sat with his on the adjacent lounge chair even though he wanted to sit beside her more than anything. But she'd come to do her brother a favor, not date him.

She took a sip, closed her eyes and moaned. "Mmm…so good. Thank you."

Exactly what a man wanted to hear in the bedroom. Did she sound like that during sex? Thank fuck he wore loose track pants, or she'd definitely have noticed his semi hard-on.

Now he couldn't get her almost-moan out of his mind, would love to be the guy to take her there. *Wishful fucking thinking…and so fucking wrong*. He had to get his sexually deprived brain out of the gutter.

"Any time. Thank you for coming." If only he'd been able to achieve that in an orgasmic sense.

"My pleasure."

He wished.

Alexander could have taken things further with her in the past but didn't regret it…exactly. They'd all made choices, and his had brought him here—back to her, back to a woman who could have changed significantly, could already be involved with someone else. It had been fifteen fucking years.

But if she were serious about another guy, wouldn't Chase have told him? His best mate would have given him an update, a heads-up, a warning—would have reinforced his sister was taken, attached, off-limits.

Wouldn't he?

*Maybe not*. He owed him nothing when it came to Sage. Chase had no idea Alexander had even a smidge of interest in her, so why would he feel obligated to tell him the ins and outs of her relationship status?

"Before you say anything else, I want to apologize for being a dick before I left. I was young and immature and—"

"No need. But thank you." She gave him a sincere smile, and he wanted to lift her onto his lap and kiss her senseless, something he'd craved for ages but hadn't thought proper.

What had changed now? They were both adults with more experience, clearer on what they wanted, and free and able to make their own decisions. Yeah, that mattered. It made a huge difference.

But would it increase the likelihood she'd get into a relationship with a fucked-up ex-serviceman, living in a cheap-ass unit, who'd treated her like crap? Yeah, he could afford more but he still hadn't gotten his act together.

Could she consider him currently? No. The probability he'd be a positive influence in her life remained low to non-existent. She didn't need to be reminded of her client load in her personal life.

Yet his hardheaded persistent persona wouldn't allow him to be deterred. He'd try his best, even against the odds, to convince her otherwise.

She blew on her coffee and glanced at him across the top of her steaming cup, as though trying to move from the past into somewhat safe territory. "What did you want to speak about today?"

"I don't know. There's so much. I have no idea where to start."

"At the beginning usually works."

He laughed. *A foreign concept*. Sage had always known how to tap into his unspoken needs, not that he'd let her know. Remarkably, she'd retained the same sense of humor, and it still worked on him. "It does. But it's not easy talking about emotions, experiences, especially when people can't relate."

"You're right. I don't understand what you've been through, but I can be a sounding board. I can make suggestions based on what you say. Honesty is the key here.

"Whatever you decide to divulge will direct where I go with it. The more guarded you are, the less I can help. The more information I have, the more accurate the picture and hence the better the recommendations I can give. Does that make sense?"

*Fuck yeah.* He'd never realized how much cleverness turned him on. "Absolutely."

The sad truth? Alexander had never given his heart to anyone. Sure, he'd had a few fucks, but nothing of substance—more as stress relief. And yeah, that sounded heartless, however, he'd made sure his partners felt the same.

Fuck and go. Purely a physical, no-strings-attached release. Until he got his head in order, he shouldn't commit to anyone. Should he? Because he fucking wanted Sage more than his next breath.

She placed her empty cup on the coffee table and pinned him with a firm yet supportive stare. "I know you want to feel at ease, but to work through this stuff, you need to make yourself vulnerable, uncomfortable. You need to be open to questioning and confronting your thinking."

He placed his cup beside hers. "I'm ready."

"Are you sure?"

"Yeah."

"Because therapy is not going to be about catering to your wants. It'll focus on what you individually need to move forward. It'll challenge you to explore where you're getting stuck."

"I figured. I have nightmares, flashbacks. Can you help me?"

She sucked in a deep breath, her eyes refocusing on his. "I want to. I really do." He sensed a *but*.

"Except?"

"I know you. My recommendation is for you to speak to someone unbiased, someone who doesn't have any emotional attachments or connections, someone who will push and encourage you without conflict." He had to give her that. No cowardice, just total truth.

"So what are you saying? Do you have an emotional attachment to me, an emotional connection?"

Her cheeks flushed ambulance-siren red, obvious even with her olive skin. What did that mean? Did she have feelings for him or had he misinterpreted, exposed some other inner vulnerability...or did she feel guilty about not being able to help? "Of course I do. You're best friends with my brother. I've known you for a long time."

"No, you haven't. You knew me when we were still teenagers. We've spent the past fifteen years apart. Lots can happen."

She nodded. "True. But it doesn't change the fact that it makes more sense to have therapy with someone else—someone who doesn't know you personally, someone objective."

Hurt and rejection surged through his veins like poison. The military had abandoned him and now she was, too. He'd wanted to speak to her, someone he trusted, get to know her better...

Sage stood and carried their cups to the sink. "I should go. Think about what I said. I know it's hard to have faith in a stranger, however, you need someone who can neutrally review your case, your thoughts, and steer you in the right direction."

He blocked her escape to his front door. "But I trust *you*."

"Thanks. The problem is anything I say could be compromised." Her beautiful eyes met his, full of sincerity. "I've always wanted the best for you, Alexander. I know we've had our differences, but I've only ever wished you happiness — and that means referring you on."

*So considerate. Always sweet and thoughtful and bloody exasperating.* He glanced at her plump lips, the desire to kiss her almost overwhelming.

Utilizing every ounce of superhuman effort, he held back. The circumstances weren't right. He needed to prove to her he could re-establish himself, be a reliable support, someone who she could be interested in, believe in, respect, someone who had prospects. Because she entranced him, always had. "Okay, I value your opinion. Do it."

"Really?" She looked at him as though she hadn't expected his easy acquiescence.

"Yeah. I trust your professional judgment."

She smiled and bit her bottom lip.

"Can you stay for dinner?" How the fuck had that slipped out? What had happened to his brain filter, his ability to discern and inhibit information? Did his fucked-up head play a part? Had his primal need to connect with a woman, with Sage, overridden his rational thinking?

Her gaze dropped to the floor, and she looked like she couldn't get out of his place fast enough, which seemed in direct contrast to her restless hands, her hitched breath, her flushed cheeks, all indicating her physical interest, if nothing more. "No, sorry."

"How about tomorrow?" Because now that he'd put it out there, unless she told him to rein it in or fuck off, he had to see her again, see if the chemistry between them could develop into something deeper. He was a persistent bastard when he knew what he wanted.

"I thought you agreed for me to refer you on." A crease of confusion crinkled her brow, but she wouldn't look him in the eye.

*Fuck.* He wanted to slide his palm around her waist and draw her to him. "I did. I want to invite you over for a proper catch up…not therapy."

"But you don't even like me." The furrow in her forehead deepened.

"I like you just fine. Always have."

"Really?" She glanced up, her vulnerable expression full of surprise, disbelief.

"Yeah." His gaze dipped to her mouth, then back to her beautiful eyes.

She licked her tempting lips, and he dragged in a control-yourself breath. *Don't push it, dude.* If anything happened between them, they both had to consent. No ambiguity. No primitive need. No emotionally fucked-up driver. No misunderstanding. Complete, one-hundred-percent commitment to exploring each other without any other agenda.

She pulled away from the simmering heat between them, leaving a cold, wide chasm. "I need to go."

"Do you? You sure?"

"Yes." She stared at her fidgety fingers, her breathing loud and labored.

"Until tomorrow, then?" Because, yeah, he needed her to know he wanted to see her again. ASAP.

Her exquisite eyes focused on his and she gave him a twitchy-lipped smile. "I'll have to see, depending on work. If I can make it, um…same time?"

"Any time."

She laughed, and it came out all breathy and nervous.

"But you have to promise to stay for dinner."

"I don't—"

"It's the least I can do to show my appreciation."

She didn't respond straight away, as though he'd thrown her a curveball, a mathematical problem requiring a research-whiz university professor to answer. "I'll let you know by five p.m. whether I can come, if that's okay."

Oh, making her come was more than okay. Unfortunately, she didn't mean it in *that* way. Her noncommittal response wasn't quite the answer he'd wanted, but at least she hadn't given him a definite *no*.

*Yes!* He tried to remain unaffected on the outside. "Sure."

"And I'll give you any referral updates."

"No worries."

She slipped past him and opened the door. "Text you tomorrow," she said, and raced toward her car.

# Chapter Three

Sage dropped into the driver's seat and tried to gain some control over her overpowering emotions. That had been...interesting, intense, arousing. Different to what she'd expected, not that she knew how he'd be, how she'd respond. If she'd known Alexander better, she might have understood his decision-making then and now.

She drove home in a blur of mixed feelings, beelined straight to her bedroom and fell backward onto the mattress. Alexander said he liked her, had always liked her. And until today his actions had shown the exact opposite.

Had his unfriendly behavior been because of Chase?

Had he been concerned about the impact on his relationship with her and his best mate?

Had he worried about starting something when he was leaving with no idea if or when he'd return?

Probably all of the above.

The chemistry between her and Alexander had been even more explosive than she'd remembered, even more potent. And OMG, he looked great. His dark brown hair was a little longer, and that ink. That was new. The sexy sleeve of tattoos wound down both his arms. How far did it extend?

*Stop it.* She shouldn't go there, shouldn't even entertain the idea of him as anything other than an acquaintance, her brother's best friend. He was damaged, not thinking clearly, and had a minefield of emotions to work through. Ultimately, still recovering…if he ever did.

In her experience, he'd form an attachment to the first person who showed empathy, like ducklings imprinting on a human in the absence of a parent. He'd connect to her solely out of emotional relief.

She needed more.

Sage couldn't afford to spend too much time with Alexander, get even more attached. She wanted to help him, as long as it wasn't to her psychological detriment…or his. She had to remain clinical, detached, focus on what would be best for him and her.

After making a ham, cheese and tomato toasted sandwich for dinner, she showered and tucked herself into bed. While scrolling through social media, a notification pinged in the messenger app on her professional page.

She clicked into it and gasped.

*Your time is coming…*

*To an end.* Her mind filled in the missing words. Some might argue her off-kilter, overly suspicious brain had made an absolute assumption, the cumulative effect of the messages drawing her to that extreme conclusion.

The sudden rapid beat of her heart made her dizzy. It wasn't a blatant threat, but the clear-as-icy-cold-spring-water insinuation couldn't be ignored.

Was her reaction extreme? Too early to tell. She had no idea exactly who or what she was dealing with, and she lacked enough evidence for law enforcement to take her seriously.

Her experience of working with traumatized people had proven how quickly authorities discounted their stories. They often put reports down to stress, paranoia, mental illness.

Although she didn't want to be viewed in that way, she also didn't want to become a statistic. She needed to find the safest path to handle the precarious situation.

Unease crept along her spine like a noxious, strangling vine, winding and choking. How long could she exist in limbo? Uncertain. Jittery. If the messages didn't stop, she'd have to confide in someone, get some of the growing emotional weight off her chest. But who? Who would believe her?

Sage ensured her external sensor lights worked, double-checked she'd locked all the doors and scrambled into bed. A twitchy, nervous wreck, she put her mobile on the bedside table with a trembling hand.

How long could the hypervigilance last? The human body could only sustain so much over-production of adrenaline before it crashed. She tried to relax. However, her eyes stretched so wide they stung. Her stomach clenched as if squeezed by an iron fist. Her heart rate accelerated like a ticking time-bomb. *So much for taking it easy.*

At times like this, she wished she had someone at home — a housemate, a partner she could turn to and discuss her concerns.

*A scratch, a creak, a thump.* Her hearing seemed hypersensitive to every little sound. *Just the house settling* — or so she hoped. She swallowed the lump of fear lodged in her throat and shot off the bed to bolt her bedroom door in case she'd gotten it wrong.

Anyone poking around would have to smash the bedroom window or break the lock and burst through the door in order to get to her.

There would be no mistaking those noises. She snatched her phone off the nightstand, typed in the emergency services number and watched the bedroom door, darting her head periodically to look out of the second story window.

If she house-shared, had backing from another person, it would have given her more confidence to call the cops. It'd make the police less likely to question her sanity, less likely to label her as an over-sensitive, paranoid, hysterical woman living by herself.

Everything went quiet. Maybe she'd imagined things, the din exaggerated in her mind, following the most recent disconcerting message.

She switched off the lamp, lay down and started to doze. An insistent tapping roused her from sleep. Sage sat up, twisting her head to the window, a film of cold sweat coating her skin and soaking into her slip.

*Nothing.*

*No one.*

Her fear manipulating her imagination.

She had to get a fucking grip. Settle down. Not be a full-on, jumpy, adrenaline junkie.

Sage's breaths shunted in and out of her lungs. Her phone had dropped onto the quilt, over her lap. Trying to control her hyperventilated breathing, she grabbed her mobile in her shaky hand and used her fingerprint to unlock the screen, her thumb hovering over the green call button.

The rattling started again, and she tapped the touch-lamp. Her gaze flew to the door. The handle shifted up and down, up and down, up and down, but thankfully the door didn't budge.

"Leave me alone." Terror tore through her, her voice coming out all cracked and powerless.

A greater force slammed against the solid wood and pumped the handle.

Sage gasped, a surge of fear-induced perspiration making her skin clammy and cloying. "Get out of here, or I'll call the police."

The shoving stopped, and a door slammed shut in the distance. The front door? How had the person gotten in? And had they really left or was it a trick to draw her out?

*Oh God.*

Air sawed in and out of her lungs, and her vision turned blotchy.

*Breathe.*

If she didn't pull herself together, she'd faint.

She closed her eyes and focused on slowly counting back from fifty, picturing each number in her head. By the time she reached one, her pulse had almost returned to normal.

She'd held off installing a security system, thinking it was overkill. But now things had changed dramatically. Sage refused to become a prisoner in her own home, her bedroom.

So she did the one thing she could do, the only thing that would possibly give her some peace, some ability to get a half-decent rest. She called Chase.

His phone rang once, twice. "Sis?" Chase's voice slurred with lingering sleepiness.

*Thank God.* She blew out a huge breath. "I need you to come over."

"Now?"

"Yes. *Please.*" She didn't even try to keep the desperation out of her tone.

"What's wrong? What happened?" He suddenly sounded wide awake.

"Someone broke in, I think. I'll explain when you get here."

"You think?"

"I didn't see them, I... Please, just get over here."

"Okay. Try to stay calm and lock yourself in a room."

"I'm in my bedroom. It's bolted."

"Good. I'm on my way."

Relief, like an antacid, settled some of the churning worry in her stomach. He lived close-by so should arrive shortly—and he had a key. He could let himself in, if required.

The minutes seemed to drag, like wading through quicksand—slow, swamping, sinking.

The longer she waited, the more her mind mulled over every little detail. Had the break-in been related to the carefully constructed threats or was it a coincidence? She didn't want to presume the two were linked, because, if they were, her tormentor had gone to a whole new, fucking-scary level.

Although frightened, she refused to leave her home, even temporarily. It would essentially be admitting defeat. The fear may have multiplied in every cell of her body like a contagious virus, but she wouldn't give in, wouldn't let this offender win—assuming it was the same person.

Three distinct raps in the distance made her jump and her heart raced to red-line level.

"Sis, it's me, Chase. Can I come in?"

"Yes. Be careful."

Footsteps thudded on the floor in her front foyer and got louder as he climbed the stairs, then fell away and strengthened again.

"Chase?"

"Just checking the place."

A few moments later, several sharp knocks shook her bedroom door, and she startled.

"Sage?"

"Hang on." She jumped out of bed, slipped into her robe and opened the door.

Chase stood there in tracksuit pants and a T-shirt. She hadn't seen him in casual gear in years, since they'd lived at home with their parents. "You okay?"

Unbidden tears trickled down her face, and she threw her arms around him. "I am now."

"The front door was open. Are you sure you locked it last night?" He held her in a soothing embrace, his tone calm, yet tinged with worry.

"Yes. I double-checked before I went to bed. I think whoever broke in entered somewhere else and left through the front."

"The laundry. Looks like they jimmied the window open and lifted off the fly screen."

"Oh." Any of the three people she'd tentatively considered could fit through there.

"Have you reported it to the police?"

"Not yet."

Chase pulled away and looked her in the eye. "You should."

"First I need to check if the intruder took anything. I don't think they did. They weren't here long enough. And I wasn't hurt, so will the cops even believe me? They don't have the resources to pursue a non-crime."

"Breaking and entering is still a crime, whether things are stolen or someone is hurt or not, they should investigate."

"True, but I doubt it'll rate too highly on their list of priorities."

"So, what then? You're pretty shaken up. You shouldn't be here alone, at least for the next few days."

"You could stay with me. It'd be like old times. Wrestling over the remote, arguing about what to eat for dinner."

Chase offered her a warm yet concerned smile. "Normally I would, but I'm going interstate today for a conference."

"Oh."

"Do you want me to cancel?"

She adamantly shook her head. "No. No way. I'm a grown woman. I can sort something out." Her tormentor could fuck up her plans while she researched who they were, what they wanted, but she refused to let them fuck up anyone else's.

Her brother went all quiet and contemplative for a few seconds, then met her gaze with a broad, I-got-it smile. "I know. I'll ask Alex to come sister-sit."

Sage stumbled back and Chase grabbed her arm to steady her. "No."

"Yes. Hear me out."

She huffed and shook her head, rejecting his suggestion straight up, determined to shut it down. Visiting Alexander was one thing. She could control when and for how long they were together. However, him in her personal space for hours at a time, days? No. Just no.

"Recruiting him makes perfect sense. He'll feel helpful, useful, not a blight on society, like he's contributing in a positive way again." Chase used his calm, rational solicitor voice — the one that won him cases but wouldn't win her over.

"No."

"Don't be so rigid. Your safety comes first, and I know he'd want to protect you."

"No."

"Sage, be sensible."

"I am. Alexander has his own stuff to deal with. He's not up to this."

"He is. The circumstances are different. It'll give him meaning, purpose."

Her sigh had jagged, frayed, frustrated edges. She couldn't sleep with a burglar-maybe-stalker roaming around her house, yet she had no hope with Alexander in the next room, either. How could she relax with that sexy, hulking, troubled man practically within touching distance? His energy alone sparked every one of her senses.

"Oh, and he said the session with you went well."

"It wasn't really a session, more like a professional recommendation." And a weird sort of reacquaintance that had ignited her dormant libido.

"Well, whatever it was, it helped. And now he can help you in return." Chase gave her his don't-even-try-to-argue-with-me smirk. "I'll call and ask Alex to come to your place."

"It's not necessary, really."

"Let me make this clear. Either you agree or I'll arrange for you to stay with him. Yeah, that's probably better...safer."

"Don't put added pressure on the guy. It's the last thing he needs."

"Believe me, he won't see this as pressure. It'll be more like relief."

"Please think about what you're requesting. Don't bully him into taking on extra responsibility."

Chase stared at her with a look of sincere surprise. "You care about his mental health and wellbeing that much?"

If she hadn't reverted to basic-functioning, survival mode, she'd have been offended. Of course his mental state mattered to her, but she also cared about her own. Self-preservation ruled her decision-making, like choosing to put on an oxygen mask before assisting others, when on a plane in compromised conditions.

Plus, her unreciprocated feelings for him still stuck to her like stale, semi-dried honey. The less time they spent together, the better. "I don't want you to set him back. Like you said, he's had a hard time, and he's trying to resettle."

"I know how to handle him."

No, he didn't. Maybe in part, but definitely not fully. That's why Alexander hadn't completely confided in Chase. "That's what I'm worried about. You're very persuasive. And he has strong loyalty to you. He'll put you and your needs before his own."

Chase knew Alexander better than she did, friendship-wise, however, she'd observed from afar for years, assessed things as an outsider, over and above her romantic interest in the guy. So, she had no doubt he'd sacrifice himself to protect her, whether he liked her or not, for Chase.

"I won't pressure him, I promise. But I won't lie. I'd feel more comfortable knowing he's looking out for you."

*So Chase.* Her brother mastered in manipulative strategy. He'd played right into her weak spot—making others feel at ease. Kind of explained why she'd gotten into the trauma psychology field in the first place.

She sighed. How could she argue with his reasoning?

Chase's lips twitched, as though attempting to temper down his pleased smile. *Checkmate.* She'd run out of viable moves, and he knew it. "Now go get some sleep. I'll stand guard."

"You don't have to."

"I want to."

Her brother could be such an annoying-yet-awesome pain in the ass. "Fine. Thank you. I appreciate it—not your strong-arm meddling, but definitely you hanging around. And for not thinking I'm overreacting."

He swept her into a brief, caring, brotherly hug. "You're not. You need to believe it, too. You're not an exaggerator. You're the opposite of an attention-seeker. So when you raise the alarm, I take it seriously."

"Thanks. I'd started questioning whether maybe I'd read into things, saw stuff that wasn't there."

"Unfortunately, your assessment appears correct. Except now you don't have to fret—Alex will be watching over you."

Oh yes she did. She may not feel fearful with Alexander Barrett, but she'd definitely be restless and horny. However, the choice had been taken away from her by her big brother...unless Alexander declined.

He wouldn't, though. Knowing him, he could only accept, especially since she'd gone out of her way to help him.

Chase fixed his eyes on hers. "Promise me if anything else out of the ordinary happens, you'll contact the police."

"Okay." Did that extend to mentioning the unsettling messages she'd been receiving? *No. Too early. Too premature.* She had nothing to confirm whether the two events were even related.

Plus, she didn't want to worry her brother any further. By tomorrow, she'd have her own big, burly bouncer by her side, so she had nothing more to stress about. *Right?*

# Chapter Four

Alexander's phone rang, wrenching him from a disturbed snooze. He couldn't remember when he'd last had a deep, restorative sleep. These days he considered himself lucky if he got two solid hours. The rest of the time he dozed, in between nightmares.

Chase's ringtone persisted like Chinese water torture. He fumbled for his mobile on the nightstand and stared at it with bleary eyes. Six a.m. *Fuck me.*

Chase wouldn't ring him that early unless something major had gone down.

*Fuck.*

He scrubbed a hand over his face, pressed the green call-answer button and held the phone to his ear. "What's up?"

"I need your help."

*Shit.* "For what?"

Chase let out a long, stressed-sounding breath. "Sage's place got broken into last night while she was at home in bed."

Alexander jackknifed into sitting. "Is she okay? Anything taken?"

"She's still wired but physically fine, thankfully, and apparently nothing is missing. She locked herself in her bedroom. Why she even installed a bolt on her bedroom door in the first place, I have no idea."

That *was* unusual. "Did you ask her?"

"Not yet."

"Did she mention anything else? Any strange people or cars hanging around in recent days, months?"

"No. Not a thing. But I didn't press her. She took a while to stop trembling, to somewhat relax, so I decided she needed rest more than an interrogation."

"Good call." Alexander would add the question to his grill list. From the small amount of intel he'd been privy to, things didn't add up. Sage had definitely omitted essential information, hadn't been totally forthcoming. A woman like her, who prided herself on her independence, wouldn't want to put others out or, heaven forbid, worry them.

"Agreed."

"So how can I help?"

"I'm leaving this afternoon to attend an interstate conference for a couple of days. I've tried to convince Sage to stay somewhere else, at least while I'm gone, but she refuses."

"I'm moving in to her place." Alexander didn't even have to think about it. And no matter how much she protested, how much she argued—because she would—he'd be staying.

"That's what I'd hoped."

"Easy. Text me her address, and I'll meet you there soon."

"Thank you." A relieved sigh echoed down the phone line. "Knowing you'll be with her gives me peace of mind."

Alexander, too. He wouldn't be able to relax unless she had protection. Her safety was paramount. It ranked over and above whether she liked him, whether they got along, whether she gave him the silent treatment.

He wouldn't leave her hanging. Not this time. Not now that he'd matured. Spending precious hours together, one-on-one, meant they'd either hate each other or it'd bring them closer. He hoped for the latter.

They still had that spark, so he'd planned to take it slow, woo her, win her over, once he got settled. However, the situation had changed. Their circumstances may not be ideal, were somewhat out of his control, however, he needed to be flexible, adaptable.

His stint in the military had drummed into him that life is short. And he didn't want to live his remaining years with regrets. He already had a back catalog of those, especially regarding Sage, and he refused to add to the pile of missed opportunities.

Initially he'd berated himself for not fully unpacking and settling into his return to civilian society. Now it had its positives. His large duffel bag sat at the foot of his bed, full of clean casual clothes and toiletries. That would do. He didn't have to impress Sage, just keep her safe.

However, impressing her would be a really great side benefit. Cause yeah, he wanted the stunning woman. She epitomized beautiful, inside and out. A bit of a cliché, but the absolute, God's honest truth.

From the moment she'd turned sixteen, every time she'd sashayed past, he'd wanted to haul her into his arms and kiss her until she moaned.

That craving had never stopped. For a while he'd deluded himself into believing he'd moved on but, the second he'd seen her, the overwhelming desire had come crashing back.

What was he thinking? He dropped his head into his hands and forced himself to face facts. Sage deserved the best, not some headcase, ex-military dude, plagued by night terrors and barely able to function. She needed stability, support, safety—someone who could thoroughly satisfy her needs.

And give her love. Yeah, she needed someone capable of it. He had lived in self-protection mode for so long, he'd become a master at numbing his emotions. Had he permanently lost the ability to feel?

Fuck, he hoped not. She'd come the closest to cracking open the protective wall he'd built around his heart. However, he'd retreated into a pattern of day-to-day survival, trying to cope without burdening anyone else with his issues.

Until seeing Sage yesterday, he'd declined help. He'd self sabotaged—regularly, consistently.

It'd become his default behavior—something familiar, something that relieved the tension, something that made him still feel like a somewhat-competent, strong-willed man.

In the short term.

Nothing to be proud of. He fell way short of fixing his compounding issues. Rationally it made sense, but knowing what he should do and implementing that had been two very different things.

Chances were he'd done irreparable damage to his relationship with Sage, preventing her from thinking him worthy of true friendship, let alone romantic interest. That didn't stop his inner caveman from wanting her, though, doing everything in his power to claim the bewitching woman.

His phone chimed with Sage's address. *Not far.* Given the early hour, he should get to her house in under fifteen minutes.

Alexander showered, grabbed his keys and duffel bag and headed out, ensuring he shored up his emotional battle armor...because he'd need it.

He threw his gear in the front passenger seat, buckled himself in and arrived at her house in twelve minutes. Alexander slung the duffel bag strap over his shoulder and walked to her front door, subtly scoping out the street, every sense on full alert.

All casual-like, he took his time, scanning the surroundings for any suspicious parked or idling cars and listened for any people-moving sounds — twigs snapping, dogs barking, the scuff of shoes.

Nothing seemed unusual...so far.

He reached the patio, still sweeping the area for anything odd, when shouts penetrated her front door.

"He's coming here right now?" *Snippy Sage.* Alexander knew that side of her too well. Not that he'd helped by his piss-poor behavior in the past.

"Yeah. I wanted to make sure he arrived before either of us left." Chase used his lawyerly, calm-down voice.

"For fuck's sake!" Alexander could imagine her huffing and ramming her fingers through her long, lustrous, cinnamon hair — hair he wanted to wind around his hand and tug, hair he wanted to sink his fingers into, controlling the movement of her head while she sucked his cock.

In his dreams.

Alexander tried to compose himself, adjusted the crotch of his cargo pants and rang the doorbell. He stood tall and confident, a bit like a referee taking charge of a fight.

Inside went quiet.

Fast, heavy footfalls grew louder, and the door swung open.

Chase stood in the front foyer, his cheeks covered in stubble, his face creased with concern. His messy hair looked like he'd shoved his hands through it every few minutes, and he wore a tattered old T-shirt and track pants.

He couldn't remember the last time he'd seen his best friend so dressed-down, almost disheveled, and out of a pristine suit.

"Hey, Alex, thanks for doing this. Come on in." He waved him inside, looking totally spent.

Sage sat in a single lounge chair, in her dressing gown, her arms crossed, staring at her lap, pouting...clearly unimpressed.

"Aren't you going to say hello to Alex?" Chase used his brotherly taunting tone as though daring her to push past her apprehension, her annoyance, and participate.

"Hello." She didn't move, didn't look up, her tone less than friendly, as he'd expected.

Chase slapped his hand onto Alexander's shoulder, his eyes full of remorse. "Sorry to leave you with Miss Sooky. I've got to get home and pack. I need to be at the airport before midday."

"It's fine, man. Do what you gotta do." He aimed to do the same.

"Bye, Sage. See you in a few days, and don't forget..."

"Forget what?" she snapped, giving her brother the death glare.

"To behave." He flashed his signature, older brother, smart-ass smile.

She flipped him off, and Chase laughed. "I'll miss you too, Sis." And with that, he closed the door behind him and drove off, leaving Alexander to deal with Miss Grumpy-Bum.

"Have you eaten?"

She went right back into sulking mode. "What's it to you?"

"I'm here to make sure you're okay."

"Well, there's no need. I can look after myself."

"Really? What's your plan?"

"Go to work, see my clients, come home." She still refused to make eye contact. *Always defiant, tenacious, yet adorable.*

He dropped his bag, kneeled in front of her and angled his head, forcing her to look at him. "How's that a plan? If you're here alone, what's to stop the person from breaking in again, assaulting you when you step outside, waiting for you in your car, attacking you when you're alone at work?"

A shudder rolled through her body, and she hugged herself tighter. "I can manage. I'm cautious, careful. After last night, even more so."

"You don't have to take on this burden by yourself. Do you understand that? Let me help you. It's my specialty."

She speared him with a scowl. "How are you going to help me when you're still recovering yourself?"

Fair point but... "This is different. This allows me to focus on something else, something meaningful." Like he'd done for years. His protection work had become a part of him, utilizing his natural instincts, especially where Sage was concerned.

"So, I'm a pleasant distraction."

"Something like that." *And so much more.*

She rolled her eyes. "Great."

Sage shifted away from him and stood. "Seeing I have no choice about you being here, about who's in my own home, hopefully I still have some control of my schedule."

He went to reassure her that he'd keep out of her way, even though he didn't want to, but she stuck up her hand and did a zipper-closing gesture across her lips.

*Right. No more grilling, no more well-meaning suggestions…for now.* As per the lady's *request*, he would shut the fuck up and give her some space. The woman had had her place violated by a stranger last night and by an unwanted guest this morning.

"There's a spare bedroom upstairs. Go make yourself at home. I need a shower."

*Fuck.* Now all he could think about was her naked, the warm water sluicing over her bare skin. And how fucking wrong and inappropriate? He needed to focus on the task at hand and get his over-eager mind out of the grimy gutter.

Before he could respond, she ascended the internal stairs and disappeared. Not even a couple of minutes later, the jolty sound of water pressure in the pipes had his thoughts detouring down that pervy forbidden path again.

Alexander scrubbed his face with his hands to try to re-center himself, slung his bag over his shoulder and headed upstairs. A door clunked into place close by, followed by what sounded like a moan of pleasure. His imagination went wild.

So much for trying to assert some much-needed control over himself. Images of her bombarded his brain—standing under the high-powered water spray, soaping her naked body, rinsing herself off, rubbing her clit to climax.

His dick thrust against his fly, painfully confined. And going by her reaction to him, it would remain that way. With great effort, he forced himself to keep walking and find his solitary quarters.

A small, neat guest room with a double bed, en suite and window overlooking the front street more than met his needs. He'd slept in far worse. In many respects, this was a luxury. The room allowed self-reflection and provided the possibility of spending a couple days in Sage's company.

Even though she'd make it her mission to be difficult, argumentative and essentially cock-block him, it didn't stop her from being thoroughly endearing and sexy as fuck. Once he'd escorted her to work—because no fucking way would he let her drive alone—he'd return to her place and jack off.

Fuck, if he had the time, he'd do it now, ease some of the pent-up tension. But he couldn't risk her catching him mid-tug. He had to try to win her respect, her romantic attention, not push her farther away.

Over and above all else, he prioritized her safety. And he had to keep reminding himself of that, no matter what his dick craved. His feelings, his lust, could shoot the lights out, however, he couldn't do a damn thing unless she wanted him to—and it should be that way. Mutual attraction, mutual desire, mutual consent.

More moans.

*Fuck me.*

*Patience.* Given his commando tour experience, he should be an expert at waiting. Impulsiveness could get a man — often several men — killed.

The water stopped, and he pictured her drying her smooth skin, wrapping her silky cinnamon hair in a towel, and getting dressed. Had she allowed herself a little self-pleasure? Enabling her to scrub away the anxiety of the last few hours? It certainly sounded like she'd gone solo. Either that or it highlighted his horny-as-fuck state.

Maybe some hands-on stress relief formed part of her regular morning routine. How he'd love to see her masturbate, with her knowing and approving of his presence, wanting him there, watching. Voyeurism had its benefits, but only if his lady got off on it, too.

Sage had tried to act all indifferent, yet she'd raked her gaze appreciatively over his body, licked her lips when she thought he didn't notice. And it wasn't arrogance, more an indisputable observation — one of the things that made certain he'd survived his time in the commandos. If not his personality, she appreciated his fit, muscular physique.

"Alexander?" No one else, except her, referred to him by his full first name...never Alex. And he liked it, liked the sound of each syllable on her lips.

"Yeah, babe." He strode out of the spare room.

"Don't call me 'babe'."

He reached her closed bedroom door, pushed it open and, *oh fuck*. She stood there in a sheer black bra and panties that didn't leave much to the imagination. In seconds he'd discovered she either waxed, shaved or lasered, because not one hair was visible on her legs or pussy. His mouth watered and his dick… He attempted to discreetly adjust himself.

"Alexander!" Her wide-eyed stare locked on his, and her cheeks turned bright pink. One arm thrust across her beautiful breasts and the other covered her pussy.

Thank fuck she averted her gaze and rushed to the wardrobe, too distracted to notice his overt attraction.

"Don't you believe in knocking?" She acted all affronted, but her body language—flushed skin, quickened breathing, erect nipples—didn't lie, suggesting she liked his attention. Not that he'd take advantage. If anything happened between them, it had to be because that's what they both wanted.

His mouth had gone as dry as the Great Sandy Desert, and he struggled to speak.

She attempted to yank a black and floral sundress off a hanger, her hands quivering. "Don't just stand there. Can't you give a girl some privacy? Can't you see I'm half naked?"

Oh yeah, he hadn't missed that. *Fuck me.* He wanted to lick every inch of her. His brain tried to make him move but he couldn't budge from the doorway, amused and aroused. "You called me. I had to make sure you were okay."

She slipped on the dress, rolled her eyes and huffed, her face and chest still a cock-stirring crimson. "I wanted to check whether you'd found the spare room."

"I did."

"And you're still here because?" She raised her eyebrows and did up the zip.

*You're sexy, smart, and so fucking beautiful, and I want to show you how much I mean every single word.* "Sorry."

He turned, reluctantly, descended the stairs into the living area and waited.

He'd just made himself a coffee – the good stuff – when her footsteps sounded on the staircase, and she walked into view. "Like one?" He raised his steaming hot mug.

"I wish. No time." She raced into the hallway and grabbed her bag off the side table.

"Where are you going?"

"Work." She glanced at her watch as in, 'stop hassling me and let me go'.

"I'm driving."

"What? No. I told you. You don't need to."

"Yeah, I do."

"Fuck, Alexander. People have break-ins all the time. It's a random event. Take it easy. No matter what my brother says, there's no need to go all overprotective-police-sergeant on me."

"I thought you said you hadn't contacted the police."

"I haven't because, like I explained to Chase, they won't take it seriously. Nothing is missing, and I wasn't hurt."

He crowded right into her personal space. "Well, I take it seriously, and I don't want you to get hurt, so I'm driving whether you like it or not."

She rolled her eyes and sighed. "Fine. Whatever. But hurry or else I'll be late."

Alexander considered that a win. He sculled the rest of his smooth black coffee and followed her outside, ensuring she handed over her spare key, and locked the house.

She slumped into the front passenger seat of her black SUV and crossed her arms over her breasts, her rebellious pout returning. How he wanted to kiss it off her lips and hear her crying out his name with red-hot desire.

In his fucking dreams.

During his call of duty, he'd wished scratching a purely sexual itch would enable him to forget Sage, cope with stress. So, for a while he'd indulged in a sort of sex oblivion.

It didn't help.

Sadly, even alleviating his sexual frustration didn't stop the nightmares.

Or regrets.

Finally, he got the message and stopped the meaningless casual hook-ups, replacing them with meditation. Far from the panacea he'd hoped for, the practice still assisted in grounding him and settled his heightened emotions...somewhat.

He sat behind the wheel, adjusted his seat and mirrors and thrust the key into the ignition.

"Are we going?" Her voice sounded impatient and irritable and his hand twitched, eager to bend her over his knee and spank her hard for her insolence.

Instead of replying, he started the car and took off down the street. "You'll need to direct me, babe."

"I told you, I'm not your 'babe'. It's Sage. Nothing else. No pet names. No arrogant, condescending, chauvinistic 'endearments'. Understand?"

Oh yeah, she'd made herself beyond crystal clear. He knew she'd be pissed with the whole situation, but he'd hoped she'd see the sense of him being her bodyguard and settle down.

Not the case.

It seemed she needed to take it out on someone, and he'd be the lucky recipient.

Her tense silence was like a mini warzone. Luckily for him, he specialized in negotiation, problem solving on the fly and navigating difficult circumstances.

Alexander had to keep focused on the end goal — her safety. He'd rather she didn't hate him, but he'd do whatever it took to ensure she stayed well out of harm's way.

She issued directions through gritted teeth, and he almost chuckled — but he knew better. It would only aggravate her further, and he didn't want to anger her to a point where she couldn't assess a presenting threat.

Anger had a way of shutting down the rational mind, making a person's thinking pinpoint-narrow and blocking out a broader perspective. He'd learned that pretty bloody quickly. A commando had to get control of his emotions or die — or put others at significant risk.

"Pull over here, please."

He parked out front of a stylish, high-rise building and turned to her. "What time do you finish?"

"Fuck, Alexander."

If only. "So I know when to come and get you."

"I can make my own way home."

"No."

"Alexander, please." She stared at him, her expression bordering on begging. Fuck, how he'd love her to plead in other more enjoyable, sensual ways.

"I won't apologize for putting your safety first, and if that pisses you off, tough."

Her eyes turned surprisingly soft. Had she really believed he'd agreed to do this purely to appease her brother?

Did she have a history of guys taking her for granted? Feeding her bullshit. Promising things and not following through unless the potential outcome aligned with their own selfish needs? He didn't even want to fucking think about that. Any guy who'd fucked her over, he'd have no qualms making him pay.

She slung her handbag over her shoulder and glanced at him. "Five p.m. on the dot. You're not here, and I'll find another way home."

"I'll be here. You can count on me."

# Chapter Five

Could she? Sage froze in her seat and stared at Alexander. The gorgeous, infuriating man smelled irresistible...lickable. That cedar and coconut scent of his drove her crazy with want, to the point she'd had to get herself off in the shower or she wouldn't have been able to think clearly.

Had he heard her moans? She hadn't exactly been quiet, much to her distress. Fingers crossed he hadn't. If he had, hopefully he wouldn't say anything. If he confronted her, how would she explain the situation?

*Shit.*

On top of that, could she rely on him when it counted? He assured her she could. But people said a lot of things.

He hadn't shown even a hint of reliability in the past. Yet something told her it would take exceptional circumstances for him to break his promise to her now. They'd just gotten reacquainted, though, so she didn't know that for sure.

But people changed. If she was a reasonable person, she had to factor that in. Ultimately, she should give him the benefit of any lingering doubt. One thing she knew with certainty—the guy had always excelled at playing into her wants, her needs, her emotions.

After he'd caught her in her skimpy underwear, she could hardly look at him. She had, however, glimpsed his striking blue eyes traveling slowly over her semi-naked body with unmistakable yearning and appreciation. It had made her lady bits moist and her clit throb for attention. If she hadn't been running behind, she'd have rubbed another one out.

But his behavior could have been a base, primal reaction—a virile man physically responding to an almost nude woman. Who knew how long it'd been since he'd indulged in intimate female company?

Sage shouldn't let him burrow into her psyche, tap into her unmet desires. She had to be as objective as possible, ensure she didn't screw with his mental health or hers, except she lacked full control—not that anyone ever really had it.

Chase and Alexander had taken the intruder situation to the extreme, gone off tap, overreacted and it didn't look like either of them would back down, which meant Alexander would be her shadow for at least two days.

*Oh God.* A rush of heat consumed her body and she forced herself not to fan her face. She had to redirect her mind to something else, something un-Alexander.

Thankfully, her full caseload of clients popped into her head. In her breaks, she'd check through the files and suss out if any others, on top of her three instinctually earmarked clients, might have a reason to target her or if not, strike them off her suspect list.

It took her a few moments, maybe more, to return to the present, the sexual-tension-filled silence practically combustible. He angled his body and silently studied her, the intensity of his spectacular sky-blue eyes setting off a domino effect of goosebumps across her skin.

"See you later." Sage flung the door open and rushed out of the car without looking back. She took the lift to her floor, sat behind her desk and powered on her computer, her heart still thumping.

Her mobile buzzed. A text from the same unknown number. Most likely an untraceable burner phone...if the person were smart.

*I see you've recruited a couple of men, but they can't protect you. Don't think they can make you safe.*

A shiver reverberated along her spine. Pricked, triggered, she sent a response before her rational mind intervened.

*I can look after myself. Always have. Always will. I don't need to rely on anyone.*

*We'll see...*

*Shit.* She shouldn't have engaged. *Too late now.*

Whether she wanted to admit it or not, she did require her brother's support...and Alexander's, too. With his confirmed promise of assistance, she presumed he'd stick around, provide helpful input, give guidance. He and Chase were seemingly competent, reliable—two of the only people in her social network she could more confidently count on.

Should she message Alexander, tell him what had happened, share her harasser's phone number, see if he could find out more? Part of her didn't want to drag him into this, potentially put his life in danger.

She didn't want to get anyone else ensnared in her mess. But at the same time, the more information he had, the more accurate the picture, the better assessment he could make, the better chance she had of resolving the issue...nip it in the proverbial bud.

Not yet. Her intuition told her to hold off, that being too premature wouldn't help. She'd do some further investigating first, narrow down choices.

The taunting message sat on her mobile-phone screen, doing its unnerving job. Compelling emotions drove her to delete the text, as if not seeing it meant it hadn't happened, didn't exist. But she couldn't, adding it instead to the ever-growing list of evidence.

Sage sighed and closed her text messaging app, leaving the ambiguous, unresolved threat hanging. Then she focused on reviewing client files that might meet the unsatisfied, vengeful criteria — a distraction and a necessity.

Skimming through her past two years' worth of patients, the collated information reinforced her initial instincts. The three suspects she'd considered stood out, going by their core issues and unstable, volatile behavior.

Trista Harvey — number one on Sage's last name, alphabetically arranged list. The woman had been suicidal for months, and a fine line existed between suicide and homicide. It all depended on a person's mindset.

She'd talked Trista down several times, but seething, unresolved anger and hurt simmered and brewed below the surface. The woman seemed coiled tight, ready for the right trigger to set her off.

Sage had worked on facilitating her to dive into her discomfort, to abrade away the mental and emotional scarring. And Trista had shown signs of progressing. However, who one hundred percent knew the depths of what went on in a person's head? What they responded to, what influenced their decision-making and their life? As a psychologist, Sage could only hazard a guess and test out her hypotheses in therapy.

Just when she thought Trista had taken a step forward, she'd take two or more back. She'd practically seen the frustration and anger pressurizing the woman like a fizzy drink kept too long in the freezer.

Sage reached the end of Trista's notes and clicked into the file of the number two suspect on her list.

Miles Knight…obsessed. He'd seemed compelled to engage with her. Latch on. The guy had joined the military young without much job experience, without many significant relationships under his army belt, and had attached himself to Sage almost from their first meeting.

She'd seen it before, guys who read more into her compassion, that typical client-therapist transference. She'd discussed it in depth with her clinical supervisor, and they'd both agreed Sage needed to refer him on. She'd already tried twice, unsuccessfully. Miles had responded as if he hadn't even heard her, as though her recommendation had rolled right off him, like he had a Teflon veneer.

From what she'd observed, he hadn't shown any specific stalker signs. No coincidental run-ins with her down the street, and she hadn't seen him hovering anywhere near her house or outside her office building.

But he could have developed highly honed hiding skills.

Sage navigated to the notes of the third and final client on her 'possibles' list. Donovan Perdita. Well, not technically a consideration.

His wife.

The poor guy had suicided, died while under Sage's care. She had never quite gotten over it.

She'd thought she'd made headway, had him rethinking his options. She'd thought she'd successfully talked him through his distress to reach a calmer, more peaceful place. *Obviously not.* And his grieving wife, Mallory, never failed to pile on the guilt, to reinforce that Sage was responsible.

However, Sage understood the need to blame. It came hand-in-hand with trying to make sense of a difficult situation that would never have clear-cut answers. With Donovan gone, no one could determine the final straw that had driven that life-ending decision. Most likely it was cumulative. Most likely everyone and everything had made an enduring impression.

Trista and Miles were due for review appointments today. Had she fucked them up, too? It could be the tiniest word, the tiniest phrase, the tiniest change in tone or body language, positively reinforcing the wrong thing. Most people had no idea about their impact on others.

Had she skewed their thinking in the name of self-preservation, her own insecurities, her own limited point of view? How would she ever know for sure? Could anyone fully determine their influence on another's life? How much of that responsibility fell onto the person?

She'd wanted to talk to Mallory, but the woman had done everything in her power to avoid her, other than the initial, angry phone accusations. After what had happened, it wasn't surprising. Sage just hoped she'd sought out professional help externally, someone she had rapport with to facilitate her to work through her sorrow.

Mallory's husband had been Sage's client, so she shouldn't feel obligated to work on the woman's issues, yet she couldn't help it. She struggled seeing anyone in pain.

Sage didn't want to believe any of her clients, or their significant others, were capable of the veiled threats or were possible suspects.

Sadly, they had the best motive. Crimes perpetrated by a stranger with no link to the victim were unusual. Most deaths could be traced to someone in the person's acquaintance.

Were her own issues distorting her judgment? Should she mention her concerns to the one man who drove her crazy? In every sense—physically, emotionally, mentally. Alexander would essentially be her roommate, until her brother returned, and even though she didn't want to admit it, she felt safer with him around.

Like a child's security blanket, having the big man's presence acted as peace of mind, an alarm system, a massive deterrent. The one downfall—with him super close and his elite observation skills—he wouldn't let her hide the full truth.

After a coffee, three back-to-back client appointments then lunch, she needed a nap. She buried her face in her hands and sighed. At least in her office she had time to think at her own pace, time to re-energize.

Once Alexander picked her up, he'd be asking questions. She'd seen it in his eyes. His assessment expertise would have identified that she hadn't been one-hundred percent transparent. It seemed he had a highly attuned bullshit radar.

However, if she pulled together her possibilities list based on her personal issues and insecurities alone, it wouldn't be fair. It'd abuse her clients' trust, encourage the opposite of professional therapeutic rapport.

Before Trista and Miles were due to arrive, she reread Donovan's progress notes. He'd seen her for six months, almost from the moment he got discharged from military service.

During his last mission in the Middle East, he'd put himself and others in unnecessary danger. His superiors forced him to take leave, for everyone's sake, and he failed the mental health component of his return-to-work fitness test.

When he came to her, he'd been desperate and depressed, unable to recover from the rejection. He'd been a high-end deer hunter since his teens—knew how to kill, what it took. The realization he couldn't meet the required warzone standards created a soul-deep, unresolvable hurt. He reported feeling weak, inadequate and unworthy and couldn't understand how his wife stood by him when he couldn't stand by himself.

Dying and wanting to die came up a lot in their sessions, and she'd made sure to do thorough suicide screening every time, checking whether he had means as well as intent. He'd assured her that his wife had locked the guns away, making them inaccessible to him, as a safety precaution, and convinced Sage the suicidal ideation remained purely in his head—until she got the hysterical call from his wife.

Mallory had found him, hanging, dead, at their holiday house in the country. *Heartbreaking*. An image she could never unsee. An image that would probably forever haunt her nighttime and waking hours. It wasn't the way anyone wanted to remember a loved one.

He'd been Sage's first-ever successful client suicide. And didn't that flood her with feelings of inadequacy. What could she have done better? What had she missed? What could she have done differently to prevent his death? How could she have successfully coached him into wanting to live? Could anyone have saved him? They were all questions that would never be answered.

Rationally, she realized she could only act on a client's disclosure, and Donovan had been selective with what he'd said, secretive. He'd made up his mind. He'd set out to complete one final task, and he'd achieved it, his last act providing him the success he strove for, in a totally warped way.

Her desk phone rang, jolting her out of her helpless, confronting, memories.

Reception.

She answered the call and pressed speaker.

"Trista has arrived."

"Thanks. Give me a couple minutes then send her in."

Sage closed Donovan's file and opened Trista's. The woman had a reputation as a highly revered doctor who'd been a part of the frontline medical-response staff. She hadn't just had to deal with the day-to-day risks but also the trauma of seeing severely injured soldiers and not always being able to save them.

That's where she'd struggled most – her inability to prevent deaths. Each 'failure' accumulated, until one small event became the fragile straw that broke the weary camel's back.

Sage had lost one client, and it had been devastating. She couldn't imagine the depth of difficulty and despair Trista faced every day, needing to live with what she'd experienced. But she could empathize and help her client develop some meaning that made sense, bringing her down from the emotional ledge.

After the Donovan situation, Sage promised herself she'd be super alert and go with her gut. If she sensed Trista didn't answer the suicide assessment accurately, she'd refer her immediately to the Crisis Assessment and Treatment – CAT – team. Safety overrode confidentiality.

But today wasn't simply about Trista's therapeutic intervention. Sage intended to also gauge any behaviors that might suggest the woman could be her terrorist.

A light rap on the door – her receptionist's signature knock.

"Come in." She put on her warm, professional smile and walked over to greet Trista.

The petite woman entered her office, her shoulders rounded, facial expression flat and eyes distant, as though reliving all the atrocities she'd seen – the sad, unfortunate usual.

"Trista, take a seat."

Sage sat in an adjacent chair, the huge window behind her desk providing an incredibly peaceful view of the sun's rays glinting off the Yarra River.

"How are you doing?"

"The same." Trista picked at her bitten-down fingernails and avoided eye contact.

"Have you tried using the meditation app I recommended?"

"A few times."

"And how did that go?"

"Okay."

"How about exercise? Have you started at the gym?"

"No."

"How about walking?"

"Locally. Yes. Two or three times a week."

"That's great. It's an excellent start. Tell me about what else helps you feel better."

"Alcohol. Casual sex. Comfort food." She looked Sage in the eye as though to test out whether she'd go into monologue lecture mode.

Trista had named the usual escapism suspects. So if she'd wanted to go for shock value, she'd fallen short. "We've spoken about this, and with your medical training, you understand that those strategies may reduce the emotional pain short term, but long term they cause more damage."

The woman jerked up ramrod straight in her seat, her eyes wild with anger. "What the fuck am I supposed to do then? They're the only things that help me forget, you know? They make me feel alive. Thirty minutes of peace is better than nothing."

Trista's wick, her emotional fuse, seemed to have burned right down to the base. Sage got that. And if she hadn't had her own recent unsettling experiences, she wouldn't think twice. Instead, every little change, any

Sandra Carmel

little escalation in a client's behavior, had her on high alert, had that person pegged as a probable suspect.

But she shouldn't focus on her own problems now, shouldn't let them skew her professional objectivity. She needed to remain impartial. This was Trista's session, and she relied on her psychologist's skills. Sage had to toughen up her cracked resolve and try to redirect the woman into more positive practices.

"It's normal to revert to quick fixes. However, I recommend more body and mind sustaining routines — continuing to meditate and increasing your exercise, enabling the two to become a new habit. Both have been shown to have great impacts on mood."

Trista's shoulders slumped. "I'm not sure I have the patience or motivation. Saying no to my emotional impulses, to instant relief, is almost impossible."

"It's not unusual, given what you've been through. Starting something new is always daunting. All I'm asking is for you to try. Even the tiniest step forward is a win. Your mind and body will thank you."

Trista shifted in her chair, as though she'd sat on a bed of cold, sharp, piercing nails. "Fine. I'll give it a go, but I'm not promising anything."

"That's okay. Let's keep the weekly appointments to check your progress and discuss any limitations and setbacks. Same day and time suit?"

"I guess."

"If you need to reschedule, call and let me know." Sage's lips lifted in her encouraging, reassuring, therapist smile. "Now, anything else you'd like to talk about before we finish for today?"

"Not really." Which pretty much meant *yes*, but Trista wasn't up to it, so Sage wouldn't push. Not yet. Overwhelmed didn't even fully capture the woman's current mindset. She needed small, clear, simple tasks she could successfully build on.

Balance…Sage needed to ensure the right amount of challenge to enable Trista some victories while staving off defeat and processing grief.

They completed the suicide risk assessment with no obvious red flags, and finished the session, giving Sage about ten minutes to write the progress notes before Miles arrived.

She hit save, and reception buzzed.

"Miles is here."

"Thanks. Send him in." She clicked into Miles' file and kept the monitor facing away from where she conducted the counseling session. Her standard practice.

A receptionist-warning rap alerted her, then her office door eased open. Sage walked toward it and welcomed Miles. "Take a seat."

He did, his smile powering up to double the intensity of hers, his gaze unwavering.

She sat opposite and shifted a little farther back. "How have you been?"

"Good. Great. You're helping me heaps." He moved forward, nearer to her, closing the distance, his stare, his tone, like a full-on fan, a sycophant. Nothing unusual. He'd shown the exact same behavior almost from the moment they'd met.

The guy had projected onto her, reading into their professional relationship, seeing her intervention as so much more. And she'd let it go on too long. She hadn't established and reinforced clear enough boundaries, thinking his initial infatuation might dissipate once they got chatting, once they got more involved in his therapy.

Sandra Carmel

If anything, his attraction, his fixation, had strengthened — and she had to stop it.

"I'm happy to hear you've found the sessions useful." Now, how would she break the re-referral news to him? Again. "I've thoroughly reviewed your notes, and I believe you're ready for the next step."

Lines of confusion slashed his brow. "The next step?"

"That's right. You've made some fantastic gains, but in order to keep growing and expanding, I recommend a referral to a more specialized psychologist."

"What?" He shook his head. "You're trying to palm me off, even now? We've been through this fucking shit before. I thought I'd made myself pretty fucking clear. How many times do I have to explain I find *your* intervention helpful? Yours. No one else's. I can't believe you're still set on handballing me to some new person."

He breathed out a forceful, frustrated breath. "I like *you*. I connect with *you*. I don't want to see someone else. How many times do I need to say it for you to comprehend? I don't want to retell my story, relive all the trauma. I don't care if they're the best in the business. I value *your* assistance. If you're as client-centered as you say, you'll respect my choice and not try and bulldoze me."

Was she bulldozing? Had her hypervigilant mind forced a compromised decision? Or did Miles excel at emotional blackmail? "I empathize with what you're saying, and I appreciate that you feel you're making gains and are comfortable with me. So if you really do trust my judgment regarding what's best for you, you'll accept my recommendation."

He scoffed.

69

"In my professional opinion, you've become too attached, too dependent. Eventually this will have an impact on you moving forward. I believe a male therapist is the best option—"

"I don't want a fucking man!" Miles shot to his feet, his jaw clenched, his face flushed, his hands fisted. "I want *you*. You're my therapist. Don't I have a fucking say?"

Her heart kicked into overdrive. "Sit down, Miles." She hoped he hadn't noticed the waver in her voice.

He stood there, breathing hard, his face turning an even angrier red.

"Please, Miles. If you don't sit, I'll end the session and have you escorted out."

He dropped onto his chair, still seething. "This is bullshit." He thumped his fist on the armrest, and she jumped.

"I realize it's not what you want to hear. It's normal to have reservations, to fear change, to want to avoid moving on to a new psychologist. The thing is you've hit the ceiling with me and what I can offer. A fresh start will swing the momentum in the forward direction."

"I don't believe that. I keep seeing improvements. I want to stay with you." His tone had turned from frustrated and aggressive to almost pleading.

"I get that staying with me, remaining in your comfort zone, feels like the right decision. However, you're looking at things from a grief-stricken point of view. Whereas I'm factoring in the whole picture from a neutral state, seeing what you need without any emotional compulsions or complications. Does that make sense?"

"I'm not fucking stupid," he spat, her comment reigniting his fury. "Even with all your 'it's in your best interests', psycho-babble rubbish, I'm not sold. I know what I need, and that's *you*. You're saying you want to help, but if you really do, you'll factor in what's important to *me*, not just what *you* think."

She held out her hands in a non-threatening, placating gesture and tried to keep her voice calm yet firm. "I appreciate your honesty. You're triggered right now. How about you go away and think about what we discussed? In the meantime, I'll investigate some alternative psychologists who can help with where you're at and email their details to you for review."

"Fine…whatever. But if I choose to keep seeing you, you can't stop me, right?" He raised his eyebrows in an I-dare-you-to-refuse-me stare.

"If my clinical reasoning determines it's not helpful, that it's detrimental to your health and wellbeing, I will have to refer you on."

"It isn't. You'll see. I'll show you." He stood and strode toward the door. "See you next week." Miles marched out of her office, the door slamming shut behind him.

Her pulse pounded at her temples. Could he have gone from dependence to dangerous obsession?

# Chapter Six

Alexander arrived early to pick up Sage and parked right out front of her office building. The moment she exited, he'd see her, and she couldn't miss him. If he hadn't been on time, he didn't doubt she'd stick by her word and make her own way home to prove a point.

And he couldn't risk that. Call it overprotective, but he'd rather be prepared and cautious than complacent. In his experience, that's when shit happened. That's when people got hurt, killed.

Cold, sticky sweat glazed his skin, and his heart hammered. Fuck, shit like that caused his PTSD—constant reviewing and reliving events where he believed he could have made a difference. If he just hadn't been so gung-ho, over-confident, impulsive. Too trusting.

He flicked through radio stations until he found a song he liked. He'd debated whether to Bluetooth one of the meditations he regularly listened to but worried he'd zone out and miss Sage. And knowing her, she'd use his decreased attention to take off and demonstrate to him and her brother they'd prematurely panicked.

From what he'd observed, the principle of something meant most to her, the fairness. She'd worn those beliefs like a badge of honor, and they formed part of the reason he liked her so damn much—not that he'd let her know.

Instead, he'd acted like a grade-A dick, like she'd been a nuisance, in his way. He didn't want her to think that anymore. His time in the commandos had made him re-evaluate...everything.

It reinforced that life was limited and to make the most of opportunities when they presented, like his second chance with Sage. Nothing could happen, though, unless she saw he had prospects. He needed to see it, too...believe it. Would she give him the time to show that? Or had he lost his shot with her?

Even if he convinced himself he could be the right man for Sage, she might already be involved with someone. He'd avoided broaching the boyfriend subject, part of him not wanting to know. But if she did have a significant other, wouldn't Chase have asked the guy to check on her instead?

No assuming. He needed a definitive answer...from her.

And on top of that, they had to narrow down a possible suspect list. Sure, the break-in could have been random, however, instinct suggested it stemmed from a greater, more personal agenda, mostly because the intruder hadn't taken anything. That, combined with Sage's twitchiness.

Ten minutes past the hour, she appeared, searching the street then locking her unreadable gaze on his.

Euphoria surged through him at the sight of her. Was she equally happy to see him? Glad he'd kept his word?

She sagged into the passenger seat. Straight away, his soldier senses detected something was up — and not in a good way. Something or someone had spooked her.

"Thanks for coming." She locked her door and clicked her seatbelt into place without making eye contact.

"I said I'd be here, and I stick to my word."

She half smiled, still refusing to look at him.

"You okay?"

"Take me home, please." Still no attempt to swing her gaze his way.

He started the engine and headed to her house. "What's wrong?"

"I had a shit day, okay?"

"No, it's not okay. Let me help."

She glanced at him with raised, dubious eyebrows. "And how are you going to do that?"

"Unless you explain the situation, I can't. I can be your bodyguard but not much else. If you want to try to resolve what's going on, you need to confide in me."

She twisted more in her seat, clamped her jaw tight and stared at him. "Really? Like back in the day when I wanted to be accepted, a part of things. Where was your support then, your understanding, your empathy, your reliability, your protection?

"You couldn't wait to get away from me. What's different now? You haven't seen me for years, haven't even tried to make contact and suddenly you want to help? Doesn't make sense. What are you playing at?"

A tirade. One she'd obviously bottled up and needed to get off her gorgeous chest. And he fucking deserved her rage, her disbelief. He hadn't made things easy. Not at all. And now he had to work double — no, triple — time, to win her trust.

"All good points...and totally justified. I can't apologize enough for how I behaved. I was an emotionally immature dick. But I've learned, grown, changed. Let me make things right."

She raised her eyebrows in challenge. "Fine. Prove it."

"I will. The military has taught me to be patient. I'll wait as long as it takes for you to trust me. Hopefully, forgive me. And I promise, I'll only overstep if you're at risk. My number one priority is to keep you safe."

"You keep saying that."

"Because it's true." He stopped at a red light and turned toward her. "Look... All I ask is that you're upfront with me. I know you're not telling me everything, and I'll do whatever it takes to find out the details. If you want me to do my job and waste the least amount of time, you'll disclose whatever you know. The less you say, the more ineffective I'll be and the more you're exposed to danger."

She stared at her fingers in her lap, pressing each digit like counting beads on an abacus — an old-fashioned, tried-and-true anxiety coping mechanism. His candid response had made her nervous, reinforcing his presumption.

Sage stayed like that, as though ignoring him would end the conversation. *No chance.* She didn't realize how determined he could be, how persistent, like a dog with a delicious bone.

He'd let her stew on his response, but she couldn't escape his questions for long. She'd be a captive in her false-sense-of-security safe haven. And he'd play on that for her own good.

The moment he parked in her garage, she bolted out of the car, keys in hand, and charged inside before he could get close. He followed, a door slamming in the distance. Her bedroom, if he had to hazard a not-so-difficult guess.

He'd let her think she could evade him by making herself a solitary-confinement-style prisoner. However, eventually, she'd have to come out to eat.

Alexander got to work on dinner, a meal she'd loved when they had been teenagers. He'd shopped, factoring in her preferences from the past, and hoped the power of the mouthwatering scent, in addition to the nostalgia, would draw her out.

It might be underhanded, but he'd attempt anything that could work. He placed several pieces of short-cut bacon in a frying pan—because she'd always hated the fatty, streaky, overly crispy stuff. When they were done, he lifted them onto a paper-towel-topped plate to absorb any excess oil.

Then he cracked five eggs onto the sizzling surface— three for him, two for her—and sprinkled on a little salt. She liked hers sunny-side up, the yolks soft so they bled onto her thick-sliced, multigrain toast. Whereas he liked his firm, well done. He'd love to see her well done, too. Make her whimper, make her scream his name.

*Fucking focus.* He had to get control of himself, especially if he planned to bring his A-game, get her relaxed enough to divulge the full extent of her troubles. He had to stop the sexual innuendo or he'd do something stupid, something way too rash, like haul her against him for a kiss.

He checked her eggs. Almost ready. Fuck, he hoped his instinct was right. He hoped she hadn't turned vegetarian or, fuck, vegan during their time apart.

He probably should have checked. If he'd gotten this wrong…he could improvise. Devise a plan B. And quickly, going by his history. But even if she had turned anti-animal products, the smell would coax her out, maybe from disgust rather than rapture. He could still work with that.

Light footfalls padded on the stairs.

*Yeah, keep coming, baby. I got you.* One day, hopefully soon, he could test that out in the bedroom, on the couch, bent over the kitchen bench.

*Enough!*

"Is that… Are you cooking…?"

"Bacon and eggs, yeah." He put two slices of bread in the toaster.

She shifted closer to him. "I love… How did you…?"

"I remember a lot of things."

"And my teenage number-one comfort food makes that list because…?"

He turned off the stovetop and stared into her eyes. She'd changed into a loose T-shirt and leggings and still looked fucking mouthwatering. "You interest me."

She half laughed, half huffed. "Stop trying to screw with my head. Stop trying to act all nice and considerate to get me to talk."

"I'm not acting." Her toast popped up, slightly golden, the way she used to enjoy, and he put it on her plate. Using the spatula, he loaded her eggs on top and piled a serving of bacon off to the side.

Alexander held out her dinner. "I swear, I'm not dicking you around. Whatever I say I mean. It's the God's honest truth. You can trust me."

Her trademark, squinty-eyed, dubious look said she didn't know whether to, so he aimed to give her more proof, give her whatever she needed in every possible way. His cock *really* liked that idea.

She took the plate out of his hand and stared at the food, then her gaze met his with a sense of awe, astonishment. "This is perfect. Exactly how I like it."

His mind went to town, flipping through an assortment of images with her saying those exact words in very different circumstances, naked circumstances — her riding his face and him licking her to ecstasy.

His dick slammed against his fly, desperate to play. Before she could see his inappropriate, excited response, he spun toward the toaster and slipped in three slices of bread.

She touched his forearm, her elegant fingers soft and warm on his skin. His heart rate cranked up to triple time. "Thank you. I really needed this tonight." Pretty much confessing something bad had gone down during the day.

She left him to fill his plate, and he joined her at the dining table.

Sage took a bite of her bacon, closed her eyes and moaned. And oh fuck, did that reinvigorate his animalistic urges. "This is great."

"Good." His voice sounded rough and raspy. "Dig in."

She cut into her toast and slathered some runny yolk across the top. "What did you do today?" *Nice deflection.* She glanced at him and popped the forkful into her mouth, sucking the remnants of egg off the metal tines. If reincarnation were real, he'd put in a request to come back as *that* fork.

Alexander got stuck into his meal. He had to distract himself somehow or risk throwing the table aside and gorging on her. "Meditated, went grocery shopping, got you a state-of-the-art security system. I'll install it tomorrow." Thought about Sage and how much he wanted her, how much he'd fucked up out of ignorance and fear. How much he needed to verify, to her and himself, he was good enough.

"What do I owe you?"

"Nothing."

"Nothing? Come on!"

"I want to do it. Let it go."

She rolled her eyes. "Fine. Do you want a beer or wine or something?" She went to stand.

"A beer. But stay there. I'll get it." He stood before she could protest. "What would you like?"

Him, if he read her flushed cheeks and dilated pupils accurately — not that she'd admit it.

He'd made sure to wear a tight black T-shirt over ass-and-leg-hugging cargo pants, emphasizing his assets. A bit of an unfair advantage but he'd take it. He worked hard to keep himself in shape, continuing his fitness regime even since he'd left the commandos. And it helped with his general health and wellbeing. Meeting Sage's eye-candy criteria, having her approval, made him feel even better...worth something.

"Um..." She glanced down at her almost empty plate. "A glass of red would be great. I've got a bottle open in the cupboard."

He grabbed their drinks and returned to the table. "To positive new beginnings."

"Yes." She raised her wine glass to his stubby of beer. "Cheers."

They both drank to that, finished their dinner and took their time with their drinks.

Alexander fixed his eyes on hers. "Tell me about your day."

"Same old."

"You don't have to hide anything from me. Like I said, the more details I have, the better I can do my job—and my job is to protect you." Plus a lot, lot more, but he couldn't go there yet.

She dropped her gaze to her glass, like it was a crystal ball that could guide her decision-making, and sculled the rest of her red. "Okay."

*Thank fuck.*

Sage hesitated, then met his stare. "Before I say anything else, I want to emphasize that I don't know whether the acts are linked. And I don't want to assume."

Discomfort crawled up his spine. The signs, compounded by her words and tone and body language, according to his very responsive, very accurate gut, refined over years of experience, suggested the events were most likely connected. However, he had to remain neutral. Let her speak, explain and assess afterwards. "I agree it's important to be as objective as possible."

"It is." She paused and he didn't say anything, silently encouraging her to continue. "It started about three months ago." She glanced at him, as though expecting a response.

He kept quiet…a strategic move that often encouraged a person to talk, to reveal more.

"I received a random email and ignored it. I thought maybe it was a prank meant for someone else and they'd gotten the address wrong. Then a couple of weeks later, I got another message, same generic email address, something that probably isn't traceable."

"Show me."

"I will. But now that I've started, I need to get this out."

He gave her a gruff nod. The whole thing felt really off, dodgy.

"The vague, unsettling messages became more frequent and started to spread across platforms. Email, text, messenger on my professional social-media pages. Then, in the last week, before the break-in, I received a message every day."

"And today?"

"Yes."

Fuck, he knew there'd be more to it. "Have you kept all the communications?"

"Every single one."

He closed his eyes and breathed out a sigh of mega frustration. "Fuck."

"What does *fuck* mean?"

Alexander met her worried gaze. "They have an extraordinary amount of access to you."

"That's bad."

"Yeah. Though it might help us narrow down people of interest. To have that level of knowledge suggests it's someone you know."

"I'd kind of figured that out already, and I've made a shortlist."

"Good girl." Fuck, that slipped out before he could think better of it. Would she jump down his throat, reproach him for being condescending, reinforce she was a grown woman? He definitely didn't need reminding around that concept.

Whether she believed it or not, he'd said it with praise, with appreciation, with affection.

He braced himself for her verbal attack.

Surprisingly, none came.

The look she gave him radiated relief. "But I want to get your unbiased opinion on the messages first."

She swallowed and darted her eyes to her laptop, charging on the coffee table. "I'll get everything ready."

Alexander cleaned up quickly and joined her on the couch. She had her computer perched on her lap and her email and social media open, her mobile sitting between them.

Sage looked at him. "Everything's there. Go for it." She handed over her laptop, and he scrolled through the array of correspondence.

Oh yeah, this was fucked. Someone held a massive grudge against Sage, and they'd weaseled their way into her life, making her feel off-kilter, uncertain, fearful...unnerved. And he aimed to fix that. In his prime, he'd been known as 'the fixer'. Problem solving was his forte.

She'd hardly waited two minutes before her fingers bit into his thigh, setting his heartbeat skyrocketing. "What do you think?"

*I want to strip you down and make love to you.* Except she didn't want his opinion on him and her. She wanted his assessment of her stressful situation.

He placed her phone and computer on the coffee table and twisted toward her, threading their fingers together. "Going by what I've read, the message escalation correlates too closely to the intrusion not to be connected."

"Oh."

"I know it's not what you hoped to hear, but I promised to be honest—"

"No, I want you to be honest, no matter how hard it is. I want to hear your opinion. I need to know what I'm dealing with. It'll help me stay more alert. And it confirms I'm not paranoid, and I'm not going insane."

He cupped her face with his hand. "You're one of the sanest people I've ever met."

"Really? How can you say that when we've just reconnected?"

"I know you."

"Not that much anymore."

He'd breached the physical boundaries, he should stop touching her, but he couldn't. "Enough for me to see you're still switched on and not someone who overreacts."

She pressed her palm to the back of his hand. "Thank you."

"You don't need to thank me. Like I said, I won't lie to you."

"I know."

"Since when?" He didn't want to ruin the moment, but he needed specifics.

"Since you were adamant you wanted to protect me. Since you pushed for more details and wouldn't take no for an answer. Since you took me seriously."

"I've always taken you seriously...too seriously." He stroked the pad of his thumb over her cheek.

"No such thing." Her gaze moved between his eyes and lips—back and forth, back and forth, back and forth. Fuck, she wanted a kiss. No way would he waste this chance.

He leaned in slowly, giving her the ability to retreat. She didn't.

Sage met him halfway, closed the distance, pressed those sweet lips to his, and he was lost...in the best possible way.

His inner caveman drove him to devour her. Although difficult, he overrode his compulsive urges and took his time, not wanting to scare her with his dominance. He'd ease in, feel his way, focus on exploring her in depth. With all the shit going on, she didn't need her fear exacerbated.

She pressed into him, like she couldn't get close enough...exactly how he felt. Alexander needed her body flush with his, skin on skin. But he'd let things play out. Make sure that's what she wanted, too. Though, it didn't stop him grabbing her hot little ass and lifting her onto his lap.

She gasped, her core rubbing his eager cock. Sage gripped his shoulders and stared into his eyes, almost awestruck, surprised, like she couldn't quite believe what had happened.

Neither could he.

He'd fantasized about this moment for so long...too long. And his imagination failed in comparison.

Before he could dive back into the kiss, she beat him to it, crushing her mouth to his, her moist, insistent tongue delving between his lips. He groaned, his dick so hard he thought it might spear through his pants.

Things got hot and heavy fast, both of them feasting on each other, like dieters indulging in a banquet of off-the-menu treats. He trailed his hands over her luscious curves and up and down her thighs. Fuck, he needed her plastered to him, naked.

He broke the kiss to take a breath. "Clothes off."

"You, too."

He growled, and practically tore her top, trying to lift it over her head. Fuck, no bra, just smooth, beautiful bare skin. "Gorgeous." He palmed her breasts, and she moaned.

Alexander swooped down and took one of her erect, dusky-pink nipples into his mouth and sucked.

She arched into him and whimpered. Ridiculously responsive. If he touched between her legs, he bet she'd be dripping wet. Before he could test out his theory, she reached down and stroked the growing bulge in his pants.

He bucked into her, desperate to feel the warmth of her hand sliding over his erection. "Fuck." If he didn't watch himself, he'd blow in his boxers. It'd been a while and Sage? She was extra special.

She tugged at his fly. "Too many clothes."

He couldn't agree more. But did she have the same intention, the same end goal? He had to make sure he understood what she wanted, and factor in any limits. Clasping her face between his hands, he waited until their gazes locked. "Baby, I want you so bad. I need to taste your sweet pussy and get inside you. Is that what you want?"

Her breath hitched. "Yes."

"You're sure." He searched her eyes, assessing for even the smallest sign of uncertainty.

"I've never been surer." No hesitation, no glancing away. Pure, one-hundred percent clear focus. She meant every word. He wanted to punch his fist in the air and shout out his joy for the whole neighborhood to hear.

Instead, he held her to him, his hands cupping her voluptuous ass, stood and strode to her bedroom. She gripped tight, her arms twined around his neck, her head nestled into the crook of his shoulder, her breath pounding against his skin.

He set her down inside her bedroom door, sliding her body along his—like he needed the extra friction. He'd barely been able to hold on beforehand.

"Get this off." She grabbed the hem of his T-shirt and raised it up. He took over, lifting it above his head and throwing it on the floor, leaving them both topless. He kissed her again, her breasts rubbing his bare chest, and it was fucking glorious.

They grabbed for each other's pants, fumbling with buttons and elastic, and yanked them down, along with their underwear, the material pooling at their ankles. They pulled apart long enough to kick off their remaining bits of clothes, then slammed together in a grabby, desperate, heated kiss.

Alexander walked her back until her knees hit the mattress, and she dropped into sitting. "Middle of the bed, lie down and spread your legs."

A cock-stirring flush broke out on her chest and face, and she got into position, as per his command. And fuck, didn't that get him extra hard. He moved between her thighs and raked his gaze slowly from her face to her pussy and retraced the path to her lips, her eyes. "What do you want, baby?"

"Your mouth between my legs, as promised."

Fuck he loved her sass. He loved... *Too early to go there.* "Well, I wouldn't want to disappoint." He kissed her lush swollen lips and worked his way down her neck to her breasts, licking and sucking those hard, pointed nipples, then venturing lower and lower until he reached the promised land.

Alexander pressed an open-mouthed kiss to her mound, along the length of one inner thigh and up the other, the sexy scent of her arousal driving him crazy with lust. However, he forced himself to go slow, even though it was a huge fucking effort. Her breath caught when he hovered close to her clit.

"How do you like your clit licked? Soft tongue, lapping and exploring or firm tongue, hard and fast?"

"Oh God."

"Which is it, baby? Or do you want me to try both? See what you prefer?"

She shoved her fingers in his hair and tugged, bucking into his face. Oh yeah, she liked his dirty talk, liked hearing what he planned to do to her. He fucking did, too. And if he wanted to uphold his reliable, in-control persona, he needed to get cracking or else he wouldn't come close to thrusting his dick deep inside her.

"Both. *Please.*"

So he did, starting off with a gentle lick along her seam. She practically shot to the ceiling. *Super sensitive. In a good way.* He returned to her opening, lapping at her surge of juices and plunged his tongue in her core.

She cried out, and fuck, she looked so damn pretty. He wanted to make her react that way over and over and over. Pushing her legs farther apart, he trailed his fingers lightly over the backs of her knees, still tongue-fucking her pussy.

And, Jesus Christ, she tasted like a dream, even better than he'd envisioned.

"I need your mouth on my clit. Please!" Her urgent, begging tone really got him going.

He couldn't say no to her. Didn't want to. Not ever again.

Alexander swiped his tongue along her folds, circled her engorged little nub and flicked it with a firm tongue.

"Alexander!"

His name on her lips never sounded so fucking good.

He continued the steady licking rhythm, and in seconds she came, calling out with pure abandon. It was the sweetest, most intoxicating sound ever. Something he'd dreamed about for too many years, never thinking he'd get this opportunity. So he planned to cherish it and not take a single moment for granted.

Hands braced on her inner thighs, keeping them nice and wide, he licked her to completion. And damn, her excited response swelled his head to super-sized. He'd always loved getting a woman off but Sage? Even more so.

She flopped against the bed, thoroughly boneless. Her gaze zoned in on his. "Your turn."

"Just lie back, baby, and let me pound into you."

She gulped. "Oh."

"Would you like that?"

"Yes." She slid her hand over his bristly cheek. "Very much."

"Good. Condoms?"

"Top drawer."

He reached in and grabbed a sealed box. He ripped it open, closely followed by a foil packet, and sheathed himself. Lining up his cock, he nudged her entrance, eager to enter.

She pressed onto the tip of his dick, urging him inside "Mmm…nice."

"I want it to be better than nice," he said and thrust in to the hilt.

She let out a little whimper at his invasion, and a tear slid down her cheek.

"You okay, baby?" He searched her eyes.

"You're huge." Her tone sounded full of awe, and she smiled, all coy and irresistible. "Much more than okay."

The best ego boost a guy could want. "You ready for me to move?" Cause fuck, he desperately needed to. He'd wait, though, if that's what she needed.

"Yes!"

Slowly, he increased the pace and power of his thrusts, in response to her feedback—her moans, her erratic breathing, her grinding hips. He lifted her leg over his shoulder and fucked into her from a different angle—a deeper angle that hit right where she needed it, going by her enthusiastic cries.

Her hot, slick channel squeezed him like a tightly clamped vise. "You feel fucking amazing, baby."

Her eyes focused on his. "You, too."

"Are you close?"

"Yes."

"I need you to come for me. Come on my cock."

She broke apart right then, her core clenching every inch of him and setting off his own climax. Best fucking orgasm of his life—intense, off-the-charts, earth-shattering, because it was Sage, the off-limits woman he'd lusted over for years.

No, not just that. He loved countless things about her—her strength, her determination, her desire for fairness, her natural, understated sensuality. What wasn't to love? And now that he'd had a taste, tapped that previously forbidden reserve, he couldn't get enough.

Fuck, he'd done his best mate's younger sister. In the past he'd gone against his gut and avoided crossing that line, but their connection tonight reinforced how wrong his decision-making had been. They were great together — beyond great. Spectacular.

He buried his face in her neck, his body pressed to hers, them both breathing hard. "Fucking perfect."

"Yes, incredible." She weaved her fingers through his hair and massaged his scalp.

Relaxing yet arousing, so right, he didn't want to move. But he needed to dispose of the condom. He pulled out, and she winced. "Sorry, baby."

"No need to be sorry. I'm going to be sore in the best way."

He gave her an appreciative grin because, yeah, he'd made her his, and went to throw out the condom in her en suite. Alexander tied the top and...*shit. Blood?* Had he injured her?

His ecstatic mood plummeted to worried. He wrapped the rubber in a tissue, threw it in the bin and returned to his woman. He lay beside Sage, propped on one forearm and studied her eyes. "Did I hurt you, baby? Be honest."

"No." She cupped his cheek and looked at him with so much love. "You were wonderful."

"There was blood on the condom."

"Oh, that." She dropped her hand and averted her gaze.

"Yeah, that."

A blush invaded her face. "I, um... Oh boy. Um... This is so embarrassing." She bit her bottom lip, took a deep breath and seemed to force herself to meet his persistent stare. "It... It was my first time."

"What? You've never had sex before?" *No. No fucking way.* A stunning woman like her... He had to have misunderstood.

"Not penetrative sex. I've done other stuff..."

*Fucking hell.* "You should have told me, and I wouldn't have been as rough, so fucking caveman."

"You were exactly what I wanted." And didn't he love that confession. A part of his primal self loved the fact she'd trusted him, had chosen him to give herself to first.

Her face flushed a passion-induced pink. "I especially love oral, have done it a few times, but your mouth. Oh my God, I've never come so hard."

A sense of pure male pride welled up inside him. But, at the same time, he wanted to deck the guys who'd had access to her pussy, the pleasure of eating her out before him. Yeah, possessive caveman to the max.

"And sucking cock?" Because, like her, he enjoyed oral, too, needed a woman willing to give him that pleasure. He hoped Sage considered it as much of a necessity, a turn on, as he did.

"I enjoy it. Can't wait to taste you. I've wanted to for so long."

Even though he'd come moments ago, her candid words had his dick rising to the challenge. He fucking wanted her mouth around his cock almost more than he needed his next breath.

"How do you want me, baby?"

"On your back. Then I can look into your eyes while I suck you off."

*Fuck me.*

His fantasy come to life.

He rolled over, and she positioned herself between his legs. Oh yeah, he could never get sick of that sight. Her long, shiny hair swung forward, and he swept it off her face. He needed an unobstructed view of his dick disappearing between her full, giving lips.

She licked the head of his cock and stroked her hand repeatedly along his length, and it felt beyond brilliant. He grunted, which seemed to spur her on, and she dove down, taking him deeper.

Alexander growled and gripped her head. She got into a hand and mouth, suck and slide rhythm, and his brain became overloaded with the heavenly feeling, the divine sensation.

She hadn't let just any man have full intimate access to her and, knowing that, knowing she'd been selective with her lovers, made this extra special.

"Stop, baby."

She ignored his request and kept going, driving him right to the edge.

"No." He held her head, stilling her seconds before he blew in her mouth. "I need to be in you when I come — if you're up for it."

She glanced at him, her beautiful amber eyes like priceless canary diamonds, full of conviction. "I am. I want this. I want you."

Every cell in his body expanded with love and insatiable lust, the first time he'd ever experienced that rare combination. He reached across to the nightstand and grabbed another condom.

She sat upright and played with her breasts, her innate sexiness making it hard for him to focus on sheathing himself. But he got there, finally, and guided her onto his dick. She slid down, taking him all the way, and he nearly came. They fit so goddamn well.

Sage braced her palms on his chest and ground into him at a torturously slow pace. For a novice, she sure moved with confidence, seemed to instinctively work out what he needed.

He played along for a couple of minutes, then before he went out of his mind, he flipped her over and pistoned into her hot center.

She gasped, and he reached between them and circled her clit. Seconds later she screamed his name, the best sound he'd ever heard. He kissed her lips, her core contracting on his cock, and he came, fucking her through their combined orgasm.

She flopped back onto the bed, panting heavily. "Alexander."

"I know, baby. Fucking fantastic." He breathed hard into her hair. "You okay?"

"*So* okay."

"Not too sore?"

"Good sore."

He grinned and pushed up onto his forearms, pressing a quick kiss to her lips. "Let me take care of this. I won't be long." He detoured to her en suite, in a hurry to return and hold her to him.

So unusual. Normally, after sex, he needed space…to escape. With Sage he wanted to be present, snuggle. He didn't want to let her go, not ever. He craved her, needed her right beside him, physically and figuratively.

Sex with Sage had been the best he'd ever had, better than he'd ever expected, ever envisaged. He'd been with plenty of attractive women who were great in bed, but the connection quickly fizzled, lacked anything lasting, lacked love.

Alexander rejoined her, lay on his back and pulled her to him. She nestled into his side, and he ran his hands down her spine and over her bottom.

Sage relaxed against his torso. She was his everything, so he shouldn't worry about Chase's reaction. Once he explained his loyal, steadfast devotion to her, surely his best mate would come around.

Hand on heart, he'd declare his true, longstanding affection for Sage, his love. Because yeah, he loved her. They'd only reacquainted recently but so what? The magnitude of his feelings wasn't new. They'd finally crossed that previously forbidden boundary, however, he'd cared about her for ages.

Not even extended separation could diminish the attraction, his longing for her and her alone, which amplified the moment he saw her again. Initially he hadn't believed a romantic relationship would be possible. Hence why he'd sought out others to try to fill the gap.

No one else ever did.

Sage had never stopped commandeering a prime spot in his head, in his heart. He wouldn't hurt her...*ever*. Not intentionally. He had in the past, cause he'd stupidly, naively believed it'd be best for both of them to separate, to cut the unspoken but potent-as-fuck ties.

It wasn't.

Alexander knew better now. He wouldn't ever make the same rookie-error mistake.

He should have fessed up sooner. But he'd convinced himself that a little bit of initial pain would be preferable than a world of agony in the future.

He'd signed up to the military and had no idea when he'd return...*if* he'd return. And he hadn't wanted Sage to put her life on hold for him, grieve if he didn't make it. She deserved better, the best.

Now that he'd relinquished his nomadic lifestyle, no way would he traipse about on his own—not even for work, not without her backing. He aimed to stay and to keep Sage, the love of his life. No more flimsy, pathetic excuses could prevent their union.

From this moment on, he'd use his skills to protect her, to keep her safe — to keep them together…always.

"What are you thinking about?" She trailed her fingers along his chest and abs, and fuck, it felt incredible.

"How much of a fuckhead I've been."

"You're not a fuckhead. Far from it."

"Thank you."

"Thank *you*." She bit her bottom lip, her cheeks still irresistibly rosy. "I'm glad I waited."

"Me, too. I love that you trusted me to be your first, and I love getting you off, watching you come. So damn sexy."

"And your inner caveman…?"

"Fuck, he loved it even more than I did."

They both laughed.

She pressed her palm over his heart and stared into his eyes with undeniable adoration. "I love the way you touch me, the way you care, like I'm special."

"Because I do. You are. Don't ever think otherwise."

"It's just… Wow. I mean, I didn't expect this."

"Me, either. I wasn't sure you'd want me. I treated you badly, and now I'm damaged goods. Not the most appealing package."

She sighed. "I've always wanted you, Alexander. You, in your entirety. Not some perfect guy on paper."

Relief and elation blasted through his veins. "Being with you is better than anything I'd ever imagined.

"Really?" Her eyes searched his.

"Yeah." He swept her disheveled hair off her face. "You're an amazing woman — strong, passionate, loving. Sexy as fuck."

Her eyes got all teary.

He stroked her cheek, his gaze never leaving hers. "Baby?"

"Don't stress. They're good tears. Happy tears. I never knew you thought about me this way."

"Don't ever doubt that I want you. I pushed you away because I needed you so bad and didn't think it was right or fair. I'd joined the armed forces with no idea how long I'd be gone, and I didn't think your brother would look favorably on us hooking up right before I left. I mean, fuck, I might not have made it. And I couldn't do that to you. Now everything's different."

"It is and it isn't." She traced over the intricate ink on his pec, the sage-leaf design he'd had tattooed over his heart, and pressed a loving, reverent kiss to his chest. "We still desire each other, but it's no longer a secret."

"Exactly. Now I realize the importance of involving you in the decision-making about how we move forward. In the past I took that away from you, assessed everything from my own skewed point of view. From this point on, I promise I'll never repeat that mistake. I'll be one-hundred percent upfront."

"Me, too. We've both matured, and we have a second chance. I won't ruin that. I won't be complacent. I'll do everything I can to support *us*."

He smiled with pure joy and kissed her temple.

"Not that I want to be in this position—fearing for my safety, my life—but I'm so glad you're here. I'm beyond happy the universe found a way to bring us back together."

He couldn't have phrased it better himself. "I won't let you down ever again."

She kissed his lips, as though supporting his words, as though sealing her thoughts and feelings with action. "I know. I believe you, and I trust you. You make me feel safe, cherished."

How about loved? Because, yeah, he fucking loved her more than anything, anyone. But he wouldn't push the love declaration yet. First he needed to discover the details of her tormentor and make them pay. No one hurt his Sage. *No one.* "And it's my aim to keep you that way." Forever, if she'd have him.

# Chapter Seven

"Oh. Oh God!" Sage's moan roused her from sleep to find Alexander's face buried between her thighs, lapping at her clit. The man couldn't leave it alone, not that she was complaining. *Best wake-up call ever.*

Two more licks and she came on his tongue, writhing and gasping. "Alexander!"

They'd made love three times during the night, each experience better and better.

Add to that his filthy mouth. She hadn't realized she enjoyed dirty talk until him. Maybe because the words, the sentiments came from his lips — the man she'd held an inextinguishable torch for, the man she couldn't forget.

She'd almost believed she'd successfully moved on, until she saw him again — until she recognized that no other man had measured up and never would. That she'd subconsciously clutched on to her virginity until Alexander reappeared, like her unconscious mind had grasped on to hidden hope — hope she thought she'd lost.

All her quashed feelings crashed into her psyche, demanding attention. And now, with the determined focus on his face and his buff sinewy body and thoughtful, honest words… How could she ever deny him?

Fingers crossed she wouldn't die trying to keep the only man who'd ever captured her heart, not when he'd just returned, not when they'd finally reconnected, not when she could have everything she'd ever wanted, ever dreamed about. Could fate really be so cruel?

Alexander crawled up her body and gave her a deep, swoon-worthy kiss. Tasting herself on him made the whole encounter extra erotic.

He broke away and licked his lips as though he didn't want to waste a drop of her, his heated gaze peering into her eyes. "Have lunch with me today, baby."

"I need to make it in to work first." She feigned a glare, but she loved every minute in his company. If she didn't have clients booked, she'd have worked from home. But she couldn't have promised much productivity.

He slapped the side of her ass, his sly smile almost extending to his ears. "Well, go and get ready. I'm not stopping you."

Except he was. Not forcefully… The way he looked at her, touched her, she didn't want to be away from him at all.

Sage reluctantly climbed off the bed and headed into her en suite naked. She could feel his eyes roam over her body, making her nipples bead and her sex super wet. He hardly had to do anything—look, stare, speak—and she virtually liquefied into a puddle of bliss.

She flipped on the mixer tap in the shower, adjusted the water temperature and slipped underneath the liquid warmth. Closing her eyes, she savored the heat cleansing her skin, though part of her didn't want to wash off Alexander's scent.

The shower door squeaked, and she snapped her eyes open. Alexander, mouth-wateringly nude, joined her under the spray. How many times had she entertained that fantasy? And the man, whoa, he really was magnificent—all hard planes, and angles and well-defined muscle without excessive bulk.

"I know you don't have much time, but I need to fuck you, baby. A quickie, against the wall. You okay with that?"

*Best suggestion ever.* She nodded, temporarily rendered mute by lust.

"I need to hear your words, your consent."

She met his bone-melting gaze. "Yes, I want you, too."

Without saying anything else, he pressed her back to the cool shower tiles. She secured her arms around his neck and hooked her legs around his waist, his massive erection pressing eagerly into her stomach.

She rubbed her sex along the length of him.

"Fuck, condom. Hold on—"

"Don't worry. I'm on the pill. So if you're STI-free…"

"I am. I haven't slept with anyone in over two years, and I get tested regularly."

"Then go for it. I want to feel you come inside me."

He growled and smashed his lips to hers, probing her mouth with his questing tongue and gripping her ass tight.

"I need you."

And he miraculously seemed to interpret her exact meaning, notching the head of his cock against her entrance and thrusting in deep. A little cry left her lips, and he stilled.

"You okay, baby? If you're too sore—"

"Keep going."

Pumping harder and faster, he angled his pelvis perfectly to stroke her clit. Two more thorough thrusts and she splintered into rapturous shards, milking his throbbing shaft.

"Sage. Oh fuck. *Fuck!*" He roared as he came, spurting his seed into her core.

They rode out the pleasure together, his cock shuddering inside her, his breath pelting into her neck. "Fuck, baby. I can't get enough of you."

She could totally relate. Normally an orgasm satisfied her, and she could move on, but Alexander was addictive. She craved more and more and more. *So greedy.* Was it possible to get too much of a good thing? It definitely didn't feel that way.

"If you weren't rushed, I'd gorge on your pussy, make you come over and over until you couldn't stand."

*Oh God.* How could she possibly concentrate on work with that image on repeat in her brain? "Raincheck?"

He pressed an all-consuming kiss to her lips, then stared into her eyes. "Fuck, yes. I'll be counting down the hours."

"You won't be the only one."

He grinned, slipped out of her and eased her still-shaky legs onto the ground. "Let me clean my dirty girl."

Sage squeezed her thighs together, already desperate for more of his expert ministrations.

Using her pump-pack body wash, he lathered his hands and seductively scrubbed her skin. Her heart rate hammered, and her breathing turned shallow and erratic. Finally, *finally*, he got to her pussy. He held her back to his front, one hand on her breast, tweaking her nipple and the other, stroking way too softly between her legs.

He soaped up the sensitive area, grabbed the handheld shower, changed the setting to massage and slanted the water onto the most tantalizing spot, getting her super horny — like she wasn't already three-quarters of the way there.

He alternated between kneading her breast and tugging on the nipple, driving her right to the brink of release. "How's that?"

Really, really out-of-this-world-amazing, but torturous. "I need your hand..."

He thunked the shower head on its hook and circled her clit with the pads of his fingers.

"More." She dropped her head into the crook of his neck.

He slid his fingers to her entrance and thrust two inside, the heel of his hand continuing the fantastic clit stimulation.

"You're so sexy. I can't wait to taste you again, fuck you deep and hard." His searing whispered breath and filthy words had her coming all over his hand.

"That's it, baby. Grind into my palm. Take your pleasure."

With his encouragement, she went to Alexander-ecstasy town, shamelessly writhing against him, a second orgasm sneaking up on her, the explosive intensity sparking in every cell of her body.

"Such a good girl." He muttered a string of soothing words in her ear, in his sexy-as-sin voice, easing her back to earth. Yet she still wanted him. If she had more time, she'd throw him down on the bed and ride his cock. She'd never felt that level of desire for anyone before. Who had he turned her into?

A sex-crazed woman.

An insatiable minx.

For him…just for him. Always for Alexander.

Later. Suddenly the worst word in the world. Later and patience, the bane of her new existence. But she'd have to put her carnal thoughts on hold.

He made sure she stood steadily on her feet, rinsed over her and himself, turned off the taps and wrapped her in a huge, fluffy towel. He positioned Sage in front of the mirror, stood behind her and dried her off…gently, thoroughly.

His all-seeing gaze met her reflection, a mischievous smile tugging at the corners of his lips. "I love watching you climax. Hearing your moans, feeling you clamp down on my fingers, my tongue, my cock, tasting your sweet arousal."

Redness bloomed in her cheeks. "Alexander!"

"I promised to tell you the truth. That's what you wanted, wasn't it?"

"Yes, but—"

"Deal with it. Deal with the fact I find you sexy as hell."

Sage still couldn't quite believe those words came out of the real, flesh-and-blood Alexander. The real, sublime deal, not her fantasy man, not the guy she'd had so many sex dreams about she'd almost lost count. The genuine superb article.

"You need to finish getting ready, babe."

He was right...again. Alexander proved that consistently. He aroused her, grounded her, made her see sense, made her feel loved, treasured — exactly what she'd always hoped for, what she'd envisaged from her soulmate. She turned, quickly kissed his mouth, then streaked into her bedroom.

Thankfully he stealthily snuck past her. If she'd seen him all big and rough and ready, she might have caved to her craving and called in sick. Though that wouldn't solve the who-was-taunting-her issue. Focusing on fun might give her a temporary reprieve, but nothing positive ever came from avoidance.

"Nearly ready?" Alexander called from downstairs.

"Coming." She wished she was in other ways — more sensual, Alexander-bringing-her-to-bliss ways.

Later. That bloody painful word.

He drove her to work, looking more panty-stripping than ever — every woman's dream man in her eyes — in black jeans that contoured to his incredible butt and powerful legs, and a fitted black T-shirt that spanned his broad chest, enhancing his drool-worthy physique. The man loved black, and black brought out the best in him.

He turned to her at the first red light. "Are you going to tell Chase?"

She hadn't even considered anything other than spending time exploring their new bond. But he had a point. "I think we both should, together — once he gets back."

He reached over and squeezed her thigh. "Good plan."

She angled herself more toward him. "Does his opinion matter to you?"

The light changed and he took off, staring ahead, his hand still hugging her leg. "Does it matter to you?"

"I asked you first."

He smirked. "Normally, yes. In the past, definitely. Now, when it comes to you, no one can tell me what to do. Not anymore. I don't care who it is. Any decision about our future is between us. Others can think what they want, but they're not in our relationship."

Sage didn't want her brother offside, but she agreed with Alexander's thinking. Knowing her man wouldn't get bullied by anyone put her at ease.

She liked that he'd prioritized her opinion. It was a huge turnaround from what had happened in their past. A sign he had matured. A sign he had progressed. A sign she could put her faith in him one-hundred-and-fifty percent.

"Okay, good. I don't want to invest in something that's unstable, volatile, unsustainable."

"I'm working on stable. I promise you I'm smarter, wiser. I won't play games, I won't assume, I won't fuck you over. I won't make decisions without consulting you."

Oh yes, she really liked this revised version of her teenage crush. It reinforced that their time apart wasn't all bad. They'd both seemed to need it to arrive at their current mentality, to allow romantic alignment.

"Thanks for being upfront." She linked her fingers with his. "I totally trust you."

He parked and brought her hand to his mouth, kissing each knuckle. Then he turned her hand over and pressed an open-mouthed, erotic kiss to her palm. "You never answered whether you'd have lunch with me. If you can only spare thirty minutes or less, I don't care. I have to see you."

Her heart flip-flopped at his admission. She wanted to see him as well. Didn't want him to go. "Same. How about twelve-thirty? I'll meet you in the Italian café across the street."

"I'll book us a table." He held her face between his big hands and kissed her lips, X-rated style. She wanted to climb onto his lap and ride him.

*Not here.*

She tried to snatch her hormonal brain from its detour into sexual deviance — and just made it.

They broke apart, both panting hard. "See you soon." Her voice came out all husky, brazen.

"I can't wait."

That look. Like no other woman would ever grab his attention. Like his sole focus was on her alone. Could she really be this lucky? She'd given up on the possibility, but could she have finally snagged the man of her dreams?

With great hesitation, she slung her bag over her shoulder and exited the car. Only a few more hours and she'd see him again. How had she coped before he'd barged back into her life, like a staunch strapping knight on a sleek white horse, shattering her routine everyday existence?

Sage caught the lift to her floor and beelined to her office. She reviewed her client load and noticed Mallory Perdita on the list. An unexpected surprise.

What had changed? Maybe she wanted more information on her husband's death. Maybe she wanted to serve Sage with legal papers. Maybe she wanted to ruin her however she could.

Intrigued, Sage wanted to speak to the woman to gauge whether she took the number-one suspect spot. Miles' recent outburst currently had him in the lead.

Once her first client arrived, she got into the groove and the morning flew. By twelve-fifteen p.m. she finished her notes, freshened up in the ladies' room and went to meet Alexander.

The automatic doors opened to reveal him standing on the footpath with a panty-blitzing smile. Sage slowed her walking pace, trying to look calm and cool and collected.

Alexander strode into her space, whisked her into his arms and hugged her so hard, she struggled to breathe.

He planted a hot, dizzying, too-brief kiss on her lips and settled her feet on the pavement, keeping his hands possessively on her hips. "I've missed you."

She pressed her palms to his chest, the stretchy black T-shirt conforming to his every muscle — and he had plenty. She couldn't wait to get him alone again and explore every single one with her tongue. "I missed you, too."

"Come on. I know you don't have much time." He released her, held her hand and intertwined their fingers. And it felt good, right, natural, like they'd been a couple for years rather than hours.

He'd booked them a great little booth seat in a hidden-away alcove, giving them some much-needed privacy.

They ordered almost immediately and got absorbed in conversation. Alexander had just confirmed he'd installed her new security system when the waiter returned with their pizzas. "*Buon appetito!*" he said and left them to themselves.

They kissed while their food cooled, then dug in, eating in comfortable, easy silence.

Alexander mopped his mouth with a napkin and scrunched it onto his empty plate. "If you need to get going, go. I'll sort out the bill and come get you later."

"Thank you." She grabbed his face and slammed her mouth to his in an I-don't-want-to-leave-but-I-have-to kiss. "See you soon."

"Count on it."

Sage rushed out of the café and onto the street. She watched for traffic, still half mesmerized, waited until it looked clear-ish and ran across the road. Midway, a car came out of nowhere, heading straight for her.

With a burst of adrenaline, she sprinted the remaining distance and threw herself onto the sidewalk at the entrance of her office building. She gripped the footpath, labored breaths scraping along her airways, her lungs aching, constricted.

Grateful, thankful, relieved. Her heart slowly eased its way back into a steady rhythm.

"Baby?" Strong, capable arms lifted her up and hauled her against a brawny, hard body. "You okay?"

Alexander. She clung onto him like an activated steel trap, never happier to see anyone.

His iron grasp reinforced his concern. Hers, too. No way was that an accident. Someone had tried to hurt her. He knew it as well. She could tell by the way he held her, the way he refused to let her go, like he thought his arms were the safest place. And she believed maybe they were.

"I'm fine." *Kind of.*

"Did you see the driver?"

"No. Just a silver-colored car about to barrel into me."

"It's okay. I've got you. We'll work it out."

She liked the 'we'. She'd worried he'd go all super-protective and confine her to a need-to-know bubble. She loved that he didn't, that he remained inclusive and chose not to shut her out 'for her own good', like a true, trusting, cohesive partnership.

"I'll come with you. Cancel your appointments, and I'll take you home."

"I need to see one person, then we can go. I'll explain later. I'll ask reception to reschedule everyone else. I should be done in about an hour if you're happy to wait."

"Of course. I've waited a long time for you, so a few more minutes is nothing."

They stepped into the lift, and he embraced her, the heat of his body, comforting, calming, breathtaking. "I'm not letting you go. Do you understand? Not unless that's what you want."

"I don't. I can't lose you now, Alexander, so you bloody better be sticking around."

He chuckled and slammed his mouth to hers in an unmistakably possessive kiss.

The elevator dinged, and they pulled apart, breathless.

"Let me check your office, then I'll hang out in the waiting area." He kissed her forehead.

"Okay." She pushed onto her tiptoes and pressed a kiss to his alluring lips, 'I love you' catching in her throat.

*Not the right time.*

*Not the right place.*

*Too soon.*

The elevator doors went to shut, and he waved his hand in between. They stepped out and she hurried to reception. "Is Mallory still due in this afternoon?"

"Yes, in about fifteen minutes."

"Great... Um...could you please cancel and reschedule the rest of my appointments for today?"

"Are you all right?" Her switched-on receptionist scrutinized her from head to foot.

"Not really, no. But I should be fine by tomorrow."

"O-kay. If you need more time off —"

"I won't."

The kind, loyal, efficient woman studied Sage's eyes.

"I just have to attend to some more pressing matters."

Her receptionist glanced at Alexander, hovering a few feet away. "I see." She smiled, almost conspiratorially. "Consider your request completed."

In the past, Sage would have been mortified if her colleagues believed she'd prioritized a man, sex, over work. Right now, she couldn't care less. Yes, Alexander was rugged, handsome, irresistible and she couldn't wait to get him naked again, but he'd also been helping her through this mess.

Sage glanced at her gorgeous guy and smiled. He grinned back, the simple gesture laden with not-so-subtle layers of communication. 'Don't take too long. I can't wait to get you home. I want to fuck you until you scream in ecstasy'.

She nodded toward her office, and he followed. Then once he completed a quick safety check, he pressed another too-fleeting kiss to her lips and headed into the waiting area. She tried to tame her breathing and, with shaky hands, opened an electronic file for Mallory.

Did the woman actually want counseling? Or did she hope to gain further insight into her husband's choice to take his own life? Maybe she thought Sage could now provide some closure.

Her desk phone buzzed, and she lifted the receiver. "Mallory's here to see you."

# Chapter Eight

"Thanks. Send her in." Sage's heart raced like she'd overdosed on fifty cups of coffee, still craving Alexander, still rattled from the near-miss road accident. Add the lingering remnants of guilt from Donovan's suicide and she couldn't stop discomfort from flooding her senses.

A light knock had her approaching the office door. *Ready?* Well, as ready as she could be with wobbly legs and an impending adrenaline-spike comedown. *What an afternoon.*

No. She shouldn't assume the worst, or that's all she'd see, all she'd attract. Maybe the woman had made peace with the circumstances and came to tell her.

Mallory entered the office, power dressed in an elegant white-linen suit, exuding confidence — not that she hadn't always looked after herself, consistently appearing impeccable, self-assured.

"Hi, Mallory, good to see you." Sage forced what she hoped passed as a calm, warm smile and gestured to the closest chair.

She sat, and Sage took the seat opposite, the furniture placement discouraging distance and facilitating clients to open up, to speak freely.

The woman's eyes locked on hers. "Are you okay?"

"I'm sorry?"

"I saw what happened. I was parking my car and..." Sage leaned forward. "What did you see?"

"A silver car nearly plowed into you."

*Shit. Yes.* "Did you notice anything about the driver?"

"Male. Around thirty. Brown hair, sunglasses."

Miles. The description fit him like a proverbial glove. *Fuck.*

"Is that what you saw?" Mallory mirrored Sage's body language, a concerned crease in her forehead.

"To be honest, it's a blur. I focused on how I could escape." She studied Mallory's eyes. "Did you get the license plate?"

She glanced toward the ceiling. "No, sorry. It all happened too fast."

*Damn.* Though, Mallory's description helped—or at least she hoped it would.

"No worries." Sage got into her interested-therapist position—a slight lean forward, open posture, no crossed limbs—encouraging eye contact. "So, what did you want to speak about today?"

"Update you on where I'm at. I've started a new job. I'm getting myself back on track." A wave of pain rolled over her face, and she sighed. "Those first few months were really hard. Horrific. But I worked out a way to give me some peace, to help me move on."

"That's fantastic. I'm rapt to hear you've found a positive way forward."

"I decided Donovan would've wanted it."

"Yes. He frequently spoke about wanting you to be happy." And himself, but he didn't believe he could achieve it. He'd been permanently scarred by his military service, and diverted his thinking onto what would please his wife instead.

Except his skewed assessment determined she'd be better off without him. Had he even asked her about it? Asked what *she* wanted?

Going by Mallory's hysterical grief response to his passing, Sage doubted it. And raising it now would only pick the scab off old, festering, emotional wounds, not change the devastating outcome.

"Did you ever speak to a counselor about what happened?"

Mallory gave her a half shrug. "I tried, and it caused more pain. It dredged up a past I couldn't alter, so I canceled the remaining sessions. Luckily I have a good social network and, as they say, time is a great healer."

"It's really important to have solid supports around you."

"It is." Mallory tugged on the hem of her jacket. "Anyway, thank you for seeing me."

"Thank you for stopping by to let me know how you're doing, and for your eye-witness account of my almost-hit-and-run incident."

Mallory stood and waved her hand in an 'it's nothing' gesture. "No problem at all. Karma will ensure people get what they deserve."

An icy fist of dread seized Sage's heart. Hadn't her tormentor written similar words? She'd double-check, but so what? It didn't prove anything. Lots of people used that expression, believed it. It didn't mean Mallory was the bad guy, or in this case, woman.

The second her office door clicked closed, Sage emailed a first-names-only summary of her three client suspects to herself to run past Alexander. As an unbiased, independent outsider, he might identify something she hadn't. At the very least, he'd give her a fresh perspective.

She shut down her computer and re-entered reception.

Alexander stalked over, looking like a rough-and-ready mountain-of-a-man, the sprinkling of stubble making him appear extra 'don't-mess-with-me' fierce. But it didn't frighten her. The steely, determined glint in his eyes and his hard, buff exterior turned her on...big time.

He cupped her cheeks with his huge hands. "Ready to go, baby?"

"Yes. Please." She glanced at her faithful receptionist.

"I'll see you tomorrow." The woman's smile said, go-do-him...now.

Her thoughts exactly.

As soon as she and Alexander were buckled into the car, he reached out and clasped her hand, holding it on her lap the entire drive to her house. They spoke sporadically, mostly menial, superficial stuff, both their minds seeming a little distracted. Hers definitely was... focused on the day's events, plus Alexander's covert yet palpable promises of pleasure. He'd already proven he had the skills to please.

The second he parked in her garage, he closed the automatic door, dashed around to the passenger side and pulled her into his arms.

"What are you…?"

"Taking you inside before I go all barbaric and fuck you right here."

She gripped him tight, nipped the juncture where his neck met his shoulder and wound her legs around his waist. "That sounds like fun."

He grunted. "Another time. I promised myself I'd worship your body, and I'm a man of my word."

*Oh.* Her clit throbbed at his admission.

Key in hand, he wrenched open the door leading into the house, paused to lock it behind them and strode up the stairs to her bedroom. He lowered her down, her body rubbing the large impossible-to-miss bulge in his pants.

Alexander slid one hand onto her ass and the other onto her nape and angled her head, taking her mouth in a controlling, heart-stopping kiss.

He trailed his lips along her jaw, down her neck and up to her ear. "I need you naked."

With his skilled hands, he had her nude in seconds, and lifted her onto the mattress. "Spread your legs so I can see how wet you are for me."

Heat rose from her chest all the way to the top of her head. Such a dirty, dirty man. And she loved it, loved him. She propped on her forearms, ensuring she didn't miss the Alexander strip show from the best seat in the house, and exposed her pussy, his eyes turning into molten blue pools of desire.

He threw off his clothes, all wild and inelegant, as though he couldn't wait a second longer to join her. She'd never seen anything sexier. Then he got her pulse really pounding, positioning himself between her legs and putting his mouth right on her pleasure point.

She moaned and bucked, begging for more. And boy, did he deliver. He stroked his tongue over and around her clit, making her tremble and writhe, while his hands wandered over her thighs and breasts. Add the vision of his stunning face feasting on her most intimate parts with a savage, single-minded passion, and she climaxed.

He licked her through it, extending the elation and lapping up her arousal. The man commandeered her whole body, stimulating every single nerve ending…constantly.

"That was quick." His breath caressed her flesh. "I'd just gotten started."

"Alexander…"

"Yeah, baby?" He gently sucked on her clit, driving her right back up to the verge of coming.

"Don't you want to be inside me?"

"Fuck, yeah. But first, I want to see you orgasm again, taste how much you want me." He ran a soft tongue through her folds, in and around her entrance and latched onto her swollen little nub.

She couldn't stop the inarticulate sounds falling from her lips.

He lifted her legs over his shoulders, burying his face deeper, and thrust two thick fingers into her entrance. Without warning she exploded, shattering into tiny pleasurable pieces. Pieces she wasn't sure anyone could put back together…except Alexander.

He understood her inside and out, way better than her friends and family did. But maybe the seed had been planted before he'd left, germinated and now flourished under the right conditions, within the right environment.

Not that being terrorized was ideal, but it'd brought him closer — an extremely positive side benefit. He'd resumed a new and improved place in her life. And she couldn't be happier, couldn't be more grateful.

"Where did you go, baby?"

"I think I blissed out."

"Fuck, yes." The proud, sinful smile on his glistening lips had her getting all turned on again. "Let's see if I can make it a hat-trick."

He returned her legs to the mattress and raked his hungry gaze over her. "Flip over. Get on your hands and knees and dip your back."

God she loved it when he got bossy in the bedroom. It had her all achy and wanton and wet.

She followed his instructions, and he growled. "Fucking sexy." He kissed each vertebra and notched his cock against her opening.

Sage shifted into him, and he thrust home, sending tingles right to the tips of her toes. "Ohhh… Alexander!" She couldn't even recognize her own voice, surprised she'd said anything that made sense.

"Yeah, baby." He picked up his fucking pace. "Come on my cock."

And she did, right on command. An avalanche of euphoria crashed over her, and he followed her into the orgasmic abyss.

His breath pounded into her shoulder, and she wanted more. When *didn't* she want more of him?

Post-sex endorphins flooded her senses, and she'd never felt better. Him, too, going by his contented sighs, the way he stroked her skin. But how would he respond once the threat was extinguished? Would removing the danger dilute the intensity of his feelings? Eliminate his compelling need to be a savior?

Alexander shifted onto his back and pulled her to him. She nuzzled into his neck and kissed his pec over the intricate leaf tattoo. "This is beautiful."

"It is." He hesitated, as though unsure whether to say more. "It's Sage."

"Sage?"

"Yeah. I needed you close to me...always."

"That's so... You're the sweetest man." Tears welled up in her eyes, and she pressed loving kisses over his heart. This guy...

But before they could really relax and enjoy each other, they needed to sort out her stalker situation. She sighed. "Not to ruin the moment, but I reviewed my client notes. I think one of three could possibly be behind this."

He stiffened. "Show me."

"Let me get my phone."

He released his Herculean hold, and Sage grabbed her mobile from her handbag. She opened her email app and gave him her summary. "Miles is the frontrunner after Mallory said she saw him drive the car that nearly ran me over today. But who knows? It might be true or her vision could've been compromised or she may be protecting herself. We need to contemplate all possibilities."

Alexander read and reread her notes, staying silent for a long time.

Nervous energy bubbled up inside her. "What do you think?"

"I think you did a great job at narrowing down options. They all have potential. They all have motives."

He handed over her phone, and she placed it on the bedside table. "So, now what? How do I lure the person out?"

"You won't. I'm not putting you in any more danger."

She pushed onto her elbow and stared down at him. "But we have to do something!"

"No, we don't. Just go about our daily lives and observe. The person will get impatient, show their cards."

"That could take ages! I want to get on with my life. I'm sick of living in fear."

He scrubbed his hand over his imperfectly handsome face—a face that had seen much more than she'd ever comprehend. It amazed her that these military men and women made it back even partially functional. "Believe me, it's about patience. Being impulsive gets people killed. I know."

*Oh. Shit.* Of course he did. "What happened?"

He half shook his head. "I don't want to burden you with it."

"You're not. I want to know."

He scrutinized her eyes, as though debating whether to expand on his experience. He must have seen her determination and sighed. "We were doing a peace-keeping mission and came across a family. They looked distraught. I had two of my men stay to try to comfort and assure them we'd get them to safety, while I went and checked out any broader threats.

"I'd hardly made it outside of the bombed, condemned building when an explosion threw me and the rest of my crew across the sand, instantly killing the guys who'd stayed behind.

"The blast originated internally, with the supposedly distressed 'family'—decoys more like it— right where I'd been standing not even two minutes beforehand." His gaze lifted to the sky as though it could give him some much-sought-after strength. "I lost part of *my* family that day. I'd made a huge error in judgment and almost killed my whole team. I should have had their backs. I should have been less emotional and more practical."

She touched his cheek, his eyes distant. "That's awful...horrific — living in war zones, dealing with the constant stress and hazards and loss of lives, having to make potentially life-changing decisions in a split second.

"I can only imagine how hard that is. But you're not responsible. You made choices based on the circumstances, on the information you were given. How could you know it was a trap? You were trying to help, do the right thing — and that's admirable."

"Is it? I made an unatonable mistake. I let my emotions get the better of me, and people died — people close to me, people I loved. And I can never get them back."

She stared at him, his facial expression full of anguish. "It doesn't mean that you ignore your instincts or go too hard the other way to try to overcompensate. That can cause issues, too.

"Learning from the past is as important as focusing on the present. Right now, we need a clear plan, something enticing enough to draw the culprit out without too much risk. We need to be smart, strategic and put the right safety measures in place."

His gaze flicked to hers, and he studied her eyes, not quite looking convinced.

"It's about balance — not being impulsive or over emotional. It's about neutrally assessing and implementing. It's about having a contingency if things don't pan out as planned.. Whatever we decide on needs to prevent the person from causing too much damage when caught, because they will thrash and scream and try to bargain."

Alexander's jaw clenched and a muscle spasmed, rippling through his sexy scruff. "They won't succeed. I'll make sure of that."

"The point is not to put either of us in unnecessary danger."

He clasped her face with gentle, loving hands and stared into her eyes. "That is the aim, but, just know, I'll take a bullet for you. Whatever's required. You're important to me. Beyond important."

"You're important to me, too, so don't do something stupid. Don't put yourself at avoidable risk, trying to be a hero. I need you to stay alive. We both need to."

His unwavering stare held so much potency, affection and adoration, she almost cried. "I love you." His voice cracked, his tone full of absolute conviction.

"I love you, too. And I don't want anything to jeopardize that, not one single thing. So you better not fuck it up."

A grin tugged at his lips. "I won't ever fuck up with you again. I promise."

"I know." She loved a smart, fit, muscly man in uniform...or out of it—someone willing to risk his life to protect his country, to protect others. Alexander still did all that, even though he'd been discharged from service.

Would his protective nature put him at increased risk? Probably. Most likely. It's what he did, what he'd spent the best part of his career doing. Emotionally, they were both compromised. However, he'd well and truly done his duty and paid the PTSD price. She wanted him to heal, not revert into that dark solitary place.

Sage took a deep breath and exhaled the escalating anxiety. "So what's the plan?"

"Wait for the next communication and say you want to meet to talk."

"Then?"

"I come with you, and we sort it out."

"What if they demand I go alone?"

"I'll tail you and stay way behind, enough for me to see you without being obvious. If they're smart, they'll request somewhere secluded they believe they can escape from if things don't go as expected. They'll have somewhere in mind and use a reason they assume you can't argue with...so don't.

"Wherever it is, I'll be right behind you. I'll put a tracking device on your car and hide one in your clothes. That way, even if you're forced away from your vehicle or your mobile is confiscated, I can still find you."

"Okay." *Sort of.* Initially she'd been flying on adrenaline, buoyed by the need for a resolution, but now the stark reality of their predicament made her feel incredibly exposed and vulnerable. However, they'd run out of other options. This strategy seemed their best, highest-probability bet to flush the person out. She just hoped the perp was inexperienced and all talk.

Her phone buzzed and she startled, a shudder jerking along her spine.

Alexander ran his hands over her bare skin and pressed a tender, confident kiss to her lips. "I swear I won't let anything happen to you."

She believed he'd try to uphold his promise, but no one could control the entire environment. No one could control the future. Sometimes things happened that couldn't be predicted. And sometimes those things had far-reaching, life-changing effects.

She wound her arms around his neck and her top leg over his waist, in an I-never-want-to-let-you-go hug.

"Baby, I could stay like this indefinitely, but you need to check your phone." His rough, raspy voice penetrated her ear.

"I know." She didn't move. Part of her had hoped if she disregarded *those* messages, avoided the jibes, the taunting, the terror, the problem would cease to exist — lose momentum, peter out. And she and Alexander could live in their own little protected bubble, like they kind of had been.

Reluctantly she untangled herself from his hot, ripped body and reached for her mobile.

An ominous text.

*You think you've got protection? Think again. I've found a chink in his armor.*

She gasped, and Alexander snatched the phone from her hand. He glared at the screen, his jaw clamping tight, his eyes flaring like boiling blue caldrons of fury.

"Whatever they think they know, they understand jack shit. I've hardly been back in the country for five minutes." His voice sounded as harsh as his expression. "Obviously they've seen us together looking *friendly*. They probably think I'm your weak spot, your kryptonite. Then hurting me serves an even greater goal. Kills two sitting ducks with one stone."

Alexander *was* her weak spot. Hurting him *would* kill her.

He threw her mobile onto the quilt and slammed his fist into the mattress. "They're not getting past me to you. No fucking way. Not happening."

Her phone started ringing, and for a moment they stared at each other without moving. Then he grabbed it and handed it over.

Chase. She pressed the call-answer button.

"Sis, I've been in a car accident. Don't freak out. I'm okay but the ambulance has taken me to the hospital to check me over as a safety precaution. If I tick all the right boxes, they'll send me home soon."

"Chase, oh God. Which hospital? How long do you think you'll be? I'll come and get you —"

Alexander grabbed the mobile out of her hand and hit speaker. "Let us know when you're ready."

"Alexander?"

"Yeah." He hung up.

Sage stared at him, her mouth agape. "What the fuck was that?"

"Me keeping you safe."

"Excuse me?"

"It could be a ploy to get you out of the house."

"You think Chase is involved?" No fucking way.

"No. But this *person* knows a lot about you and your life. Who's to say they didn't ram into your brother on purpose, knowing you'd want to see him. If you're all flustered and vulnerable, you'll be easy to kidnap or attack...presumably both."

She started trembling and couldn't stop. "So, what now?"

"When your brother's got the green light for discharge, I'll go get him."

"You're going to leave me alone? Shouldn't I come with you?"

"Too dangerous. Too easy to separate us and lure you away."

She tried to swallow the boulder of stress blocking her throat. "It's unsafe here, too. They've broken into my house before. They could do it again."

"That would be pretty bold and extra difficult now that you've got the additional security measures in place."

"I suppose." She wanted to believe it, yet confidence drained from her like dirty dishwater down the plughole.

"Lock yourself in your bedroom and keep your phone on you. If you hear anything, call triple zero, then me. Got it?"

Her heart wouldn't stop racing, her stomach roiled, her skin turned clammy. If her body didn't settle, she'd be taken to hospital next. She tried to swallow the huge lump of anxiety swelling in her throat. "I think so."

He held her face, his gaze locking on her eyes. "No 'I think so'. I need a definite *yes*."

"Yes."

"Good. I'm going to grab the trackers from my place. I won't be gone long." He swung out of bed, pulled on his jeans and T-shirt and flew out of the house, a man on a no-time-to-waste mission.

Sage threw on her robe and locked the door behind him. She stood there, frozen, and hugged her arms around herself. This sucked.

Thankfully, within thirty minutes, he returned. Even in that short time, she'd missed him.

She heard him fiddling around with her car, then he strode inside and shut the door. Sage stood at the top of the stairs, and he charged up, reached for her and wrapped her in his arms. "You okay?"

"Fine." *Kind of.*

"Anything weird happen? Anything at all?" He pulled away and studied her eyes.

"No."

"Good." He planted a hard kiss on her lips, then held her hand and led her back into the bedroom. "Let's get this tracker secured inside your bra."

Alexander grabbed the lacy one he had flung onto the floor earlier in their haste to fuck and requested she put it back on. She did, her hands shaky, fumbling with the clasp. Alexander took over, his fingers becoming a welcome distraction. No, much, much more than that.

Purposeful.

Driven.

She hungered for his warm, arousing, adoring touch.

He installed the tiny bug in among her underwire, and she could barely feel the thing. The chances of someone discovering it were remote, unless they had experience in the field.

Like Miles.

Like Trista.

She shivered.

He ran his palms along her arms and looked her in the eye. "You're all set. The second I go, you lock me out and stay home. And keep your mobile on you at all times. Understand?"

She nodded. "Yes."

Alexander cupped her face. "It's all going to work out, okay?"

"I hope so."

"Do you trust me?"

"Of course. It's everyone else... Well, except my brother."

Her phone rang. "It's Chase," she said and pressed the green call-answer button. "How are you doing?"

"Ready to go home."

"You can stay at my place."

"Thanks, but I'm fine. They've given me a cleaner than clean bill of health."

"That's great." She swallowed the bulge of nerves balled in her throat and darted her gaze to her man.

He nodded.

"Where should Alexander pick you up?"

"Just Alexander? Is everything okay?"

"Yes. What's the address?"

Chase hesitated, then recited the details. She repeated the info aloud, allowing her man to type it into his phone.

She hung up and turned to the guy she loved. "He's ready."

"Are you?"

"I don't have a choice. Like you said, you shouldn't take too long. And I have the bra tracker, so unless the person gets me naked, we should be fine." She needed to inject some humor into the conversation or risk drowning in a deluge of distress.

He stroked her very responsive nipple. "Good point."

"Pity you have to leave now then."

"Massive disappointment. But my best friend needs me."

"He does. Go. I'm good."

Alexander held her plastered to him and smashed his mouth to hers in a kiln-hot kiss. "See you soon, baby."

She locked up behind him, rechecked all the doors and windows, activated the alarm and bolted herself in her bedroom. She put the TV on low…and couldn't concentrate. Until Alexander arrived, she'd sit on that scary, treacherous, emotional edge.

Her phone rang and she answered, shoving it to her ear before even checking the caller ID. "Alexander?"

# Chapter Nine

"No...Mallory. Sorry to call you out of hours, but you did encourage Donovan to ring if it was an emergency — and I think this qualifies."

She paused, the suspense filling Sage's stomach with panic. "On the way home from work I saw a man hanging around your office building. He looked a lot like the guy that nearly ran you over the other day."

Sage's breath caught in her airway. She tried to keep her voice in check, while attempting to resettle her heart into a normal-ish rhythm, tried not to sound as shaken as she felt. "I see. I appreciate you letting me know."

Oh God, why had Miles gone to her work? Was he on some bender? Had he lost the plot, taken a skydive from sanity, well and truly flipped?

Part of her wanted to speak to him, talk him down, and part of her was petrified.

"I'll leave you to it. Just thought I should say something."

"Yes, thank you."

They hung up and, a few minutes later, she received an alert. Anxiety surged through her body, slicing through her nerves like a blunt knife. Someone had entered her office building without authorization.

Had Miles broken in? What did he hope to achieve? Get her out of her comfort zone? Out of the safety of her home?

The ringtone blared from her phone, the security firm's number flashing on the screen. She answered with a quivering hand. "Sage speaking."

"Your office alarm has been activated. Are you able to meet us onsite? We need to confirm whether this is a break-in, a fault or a staff member forgetting the code."

"Yes. Um...I'll see you in about twenty-five minutes." Hopefully, they'd beat her there and catch the culprit.

Sage called Alexander to let him know the situation, and his phone rang and rang and went to voicemail. She left a message and waited.

Ten minutes passed with no reply from her man, so she got dressed and rushed to her workplace. She parked in between two cars, jumped out, slammed the door shut and pressed her key-fob to engage the central locking.

Before she could even turn around, a sharp jab pierced her neck. Sage smacked her hand onto the injection site and tried to run. She only took a couple of staggered steps and collapsed.

"What...?" Her voice lost energy, coming out as an indecipherable whisper. "Alex...?"

"He can't help you now." A grim, gloating tone echoed in her ears right before she blacked out.

\* \* \* \*

"You're awake." Mallory's eyes met hers in the rearview mirror, her deranged smile sending a shudder of fear through Sage's immobilized body.

Darkness crowded her like walls closing in, the occasional streetlight flickering overhead. How long had she been unconscious? Her stomach churned and her pulse spiked, her heart rate hitting stroke territory.

Sage tried to take controlled breaths but could barely manage short, shallow gasps. Dizziness made her head spin. She needed more time to think. She needed Alexander. He'd know what to do.

*Please find me.*

The car stopped, and the back door swung open. Mallory reached in, yanked her to the edge of the seat and unlocked the cuffs cutting into Sage's chafed ankles. "Get up."

Pins and needles pricked and tingled through Sage's toes all the way to her calves, the slightest knock sending a lightning bolt of electricity to her temporarily deadened nerve endings.

A sensor light splashed over the car and tree-lined, secluded surroundings. She pressed her buzzy feet on the dirt driveway. Dirt? Definitely not local suburbia, though it didn't mean they were far away. Some bigger blocks were less than an hour's drive from Melbourne.

Dusk had almost descended into night by the time Mallory had attacked her, cloaking them from prying eyes and keeping Mallory's intentions hidden.

Not even the security guys had had a chance to see her, see them. Given it would be way past the twenty-five-minute mark, security should soon twig that she'd abandoned her car in the parking lot and call the police.

Fingers crossed.

Mallory grabbed Sage's arm and wrenched her out of the car. Sage stumbled and bumped into the grief-stricken, crazed woman, sending a shock of tickly tingles the length of her legs.

Surprisingly, Mallory steadied her — probably because it would be a hell of a lot harder to lug her up from the ground a second time.

"Come on." Mallory dragged her onto a trail leading to the rear of a farm-style house with a wrap-around veranda and porch swing. Such a sweet, serene scene, in contrast to the stark reality.

A shiver shook through her body. Although not cold, her teeth chattered, and goosebumps rose on her skin.

Focus. She had to assess the area and determine possible escape routes. A mini forest stretched out to the left, and the back of the property extended into paddocks. Where they led, she had no clue, but she'd give any opportunity a go.

Mallory stopped suddenly, right in front of a huge, sturdy oak tree, with a noose hanging down and a wooden stepladder underneath, a gun on the ground to her left.

Sage's heart thumped in her throat, and she struggled to suck in oxygen like air through a bent straw. "What's this?" Her voice came out cracked and softer than a whisper.

"Where you say goodbye. No, farewell." She nudged Sage forward.

"Hang on, hang on. Is this where you found your husband?"

"So smart. Pity it's too late to put two and two together." Mallory pushed her a few steps closer.

"Wait! Listen to me —"

"Like my husband did? No thanks."

"Donovan was troubled. That's why he chose to see a psychologist."

"Are you blaming the victim now?"

*Shit*, she had to tread super carefully, like tiptoeing through a minefield. "No. I'm trying to put the situation into perspective. He struggled with demons that no one could exorcise."

"You mean *you* couldn't."

"I couldn't, you couldn't, he couldn't. Believe me, I wanted to pull him out of that dark, desperate place, but he'd fallen into a deep pit of depression and couldn't find a way to climb out. Though, he tried."

"Not enough. Maybe if he'd had the right encouragement…"

Sage looked the woman in the eye. She had to make it about Mallory to delay things, to increase her chances of surviving. "What encouragement do *you* need? What will it take to help *you* heal?"

# Chapter Ten

Alexander dropped Chase at his home, got him settled and returned to Sage's place in the best mood ever. His closest friend was fine, and now, if all went to plan, he could celebrate all night with his woman.

He parked in the driveway and entered through the front door, eager to rejoin her in bed. "Sage?" He strode into the bedroom, the covers thrown aside, the place pin-drop quiet. No fucking sign of her.

Maybe in the en suite? "Sage! Where are you, babe?" He searched the whole house, stomping from room to room and…

Empty.

She'd gone.

Fucking gone. He shoved both his hands in his hair and tried to breathe. Tried to get the required oxygen levels into his lungs.

Why?

Where?

She'd promised to stay put. What had made her change her mind? Had to be something significant if she'd left of her own volition. Unless she'd been kidnapped?

*Fuck.*

He breathed out hard and tried to hold himself together, which was difficult as all fuck when images of his past kept barraging his brain — negative, life-ending images that still haunted him. He'd just reconnected with her, reconciled. No way could he lose her now. No fucking way.

Garage. Was her car there? He rushed to check.

Nope. Wherever she'd gone, she'd taken her car, or someone had taken her in it.

Tracker.

*Yes.*

He could find out where she'd headed, where she was assuming the devices hadn't been intercepted. The likelihood remained small unless the person behind the threats had a special military or police background. The perp had to know how to do a thorough sweep. Some of her clients may understand what to look for. He had everything crossed the dude didn't.

Alexander whipped his phone out and *shit*. She'd called and left a message. He'd put his mobile on silent in the hospital and got distracted getting her brother sorted. He had a listen and *fuck. Fuck*!

Logging into his tracker app, he quickly determined her car had been ditched by her work, but her bra tracker took her into the outer north-eastern suburbs of Melbourne. The spot had remained static for several minutes, making his blood pressure shoot through the roof.

He jumped into his car and sped, following the trail, hoping he wasn't too late. His pulse pounded, and he broke out into a sweat. It was the longest, most nerve-wracking drive of his life.

Alexander parked in the street, out front of a charming, picturesque property. The whole thing looked wrong, incongruent, kind of like a clown. That fake, painted-on smile seeming to hide inner darkness…evil. He fucking hated clowns.

He crept along the dirt driveway, distant voices drifting to him. Next to the kidnapper's silver car, he grabbed some discarded handcuffs, ready to restrain the prick. Using his commando skills, he charged forward, in the quietest way possible, following the track into a large backyard.

His beautiful Sage stood under an enormous tree, her hands behind her back, a stepladder in front of her and Mallory standing at her side.

*Mallory, not Miles.*

*Fuck me.* She'd set the guy up.

As he got closer, a noose came into view.

*Holy fuck.*

The woman grabbed the knotted loop and went to place it over Sage's head. He ran toward them. "Sage!"

Mallory dropped the rope, and she and his girl both glanced at him with equal and opposite reactions. Sage looked ecstatic, thankful, while the other woman appeared beyond distraught, beyond pissed off.

Sage wasted no time, kicking out and knocking her tormentor down, then made a run for it, diving straight into his arms. He'd never felt so relieved.

"Where do you think you're going?"

They jerked their heads up, and Mallory approached with a shotgun drawn, her hand shaking. *Not a good sign*. Far *from a good sign. A fucking* lethal *sign*.

"Put the gun down," Alexander said in his calmest, hostage-negotiator voice.

"You spoiled my plans." She kept coming closer, still pointing that fucking hunting rifle.

"It doesn't have to end this way. I can get you some help. You haven't hurt anyone. You have options." His girl had used the perfect bargaining tactic. Fuck, he loved her.

"You killed someone and got away with it." Mallory's acerbic tone was tinged with cutting pain.

"As awful and confronting as it is to comprehend, your husband hurt himself."

Mallory moved nearer, waving the weapon at them, her finger on the trigger. "You'd determined he had chronic depression. Why didn't you stop him? His death ruined my life."

The on-edge woman shook her head and kept the gun pointed in their direction. "Donovan dying... It shouldn't have happened. That horrible image haunts me day and night. It's etched into my brain. Then knowing he didn't want to live, not even for me!"

Her glare slammed onto them, and she stopped a meter away. "And because the coroner 'confirmed' he'd killed himself, his life insurance became null and void, and they wouldn't pay out a cent. Not one cent. See what you've done?" She aimed the firearm right at Sage's heart.

He had to do something and fast. Distract, in order to disarm the unstable woman. "Is that sirens?" Alexander stared over her shoulder, toward the front of the farmhouse.

Mallory whirled around to follow his gaze.

Before he could move, Sage kicked the gun out of the woman's hand, and it fired. Mallory stumbled and cried out, and he took the off-guard opportunity to tackle her to the ground. He darted his gaze to his girl. She remained upright. No visible signs of blood. She looked fine. Unhurt...physically. Fucking impressive move.

Sage toed the gun out of reach.

His eyes zeroed in on his woman's. "You okay?"

She nodded. "Okay as I can be."

Sage looked exhausted and, going by his deployment experience, once the adrenaline pumping into her system dissipated, she'd crash. And he'd be there for her, like he intended to be, eternally.

Except he wasn't exempt, either. He expected to come down pretty hard, pretty soon. *Not yet. Not while still in soldier mode.* First he needed to ensure Mallory got taken into custody. Second, he needed Sage safe in his arms.

Mallory screamed and attempted to fight, thrashing and bucking. Alexander gripped her wrists, immobilizing any retaliation, any scratching attempts, and levered her into standing.

He led her to the house and cuffed her to a porch pole by the back door.

Mallory continued to try to break free but...not happening. He stepped away from her, perspiration pouring down his chest and back, pulled his mobile out of his pocket and called the cops, giving them a general overview and the coordinates of where to find them. Now that the threat had gotten sorted and he'd organized the practical stuff, he could revert to civilian mode.

He spun toward Sage, who hovered nearby. She looked wrecked but so fucking beautiful. No matter what Mallory thought, Sage had never been her nemesis — quite the opposite.

In the end, Donovan killing himself had ended two lives, his as well as his wife's. Not literally, however, his actions definitely had a flow-on effect. She'd most likely be jailed for a long time. If not quantity, she'd at least lose her quality of life.

The main thing was he and Sage were safe, alive. The crisis averted because of their teamwork.

He stared at his exquisite woman. "Turn around."

She did as he asked.

Alexander retrieved the handcuff key from Mallory's pants pocket and undid Sage's shackles, the metal clanging onto the concrete. She brought her hands in front of her and rubbed her red-raw wrists. He took over, trying to soothe her, trying to abolish any memories, any remnants from the past few traumatic hours, days, weeks.

Sirens sounded in the distance, the wailing growing louder as the cops, and possibly ambulance, approached. Elated didn't even come close to portraying how he felt, more like lucky, grateful, optimistic. Although the circumstances were extreme, stressful, life-threatening — the absolute opposite of romantic — he'd never believed more in the possibility of a happily-ever-after.

The rest of the night happened in a clichéd blur. The police arrived, bombarded them with questions and hauled Mallory off. He'd hardly had a chance to speak to Sage, check in with how she'd been coping.

Relief quickly turned to 'what ifs' that could drive a person crazy. He'd been there, more than done that.

And he'd do everything he could to talk Sage through it and prevent her descending down that unhelpful rabbit-hole of emotional negativity.

Thankfully, she had regular psychologist supervision, someone professional to speak to, someone external to what had happened to problem solve through it, put the whole thing in some sort of meaningful, palatable perspective.

Alexander negotiated to take her home now, promising they'd return to the police station in the morning to answer any more questions and give a formal statement.

Sage sat silent for the whole drive, and he respected that. He knew all about the importance of having time to process outcomes. He'd give her all the space she needed...within reason, because avoiding wouldn't help address any lingering issues either. It came down to balance.

Before he'd clicked her seatbelt into place and they'd left, Sage agreed to collect her car the next day. Neither of them had the energy nor motivation to do it tonight. The fight-and-flight chemicals had worn off, leaving them both thoroughly fatigued.

Shattered.

They needed to get home and rest, twined together in bed. They needed some chill time to relax and rejuvenate.

Refresh. Recuperate.

Home. No longer purely a place to reside. *Wherever Sage was* had become his new definition. Being with her reinforced that home was a feeling, a safe haven, a sense of peace that a physical structure alone couldn't provide.

He parked in her garage and turned to her. She stared out of her window as though focused inwardly, unaware of her surroundings, probably replaying everything in her mind, which could fuck with a person, make them fixate on something out of their control.

Alexander ran his palm gently over her closest arm, and she twisted to face him. He could practically see her pulse thumping in her neck like she'd been jolted awake from a deep sleep. "Let's go inside."

She frowned and nodded, like she'd just realized where they were. He sprang out of the car and hurried to the passenger side, ready to assist if she'd zoned out. Chances were her body would be weak, unsteady, in shock. He needed to get her showered, clean off all the grime of the day and into bed…with him.

He'd emphasize he'd protect her, keep her safe and secure, help her heal — shower her with his undying, irrefutable love.

She took his hand, and, the second they stepped into the front foyer, he whisked her into his arms. He expected a protest, but she clutched onto him like a koala gripping tight to a windblown eucalyptus tree.

He climbed the stairs and set her down in her en suite, holding her in a loose embrace. She needed to know he'd always be available when she required him.

Sage's glorious golden eyes met his. "Thank you."

"You don't need to thank me. You're mine, understand that? I'm never letting you go." Emotionally, metaphorically, they'd remain tethered. He'd make sure of it.

She hugged him with an unyielding ferocity, their bodies flush, no space between them.

Physically, he couldn't always keep her close, even if he wanted to. It wasn't feasible. But, thank fuck, he'd have her soft, sweet, sexy body to look forward to every day, every night.

Now he had to focus on pragmatic considerations. Get Sage nice and clean, for her to then get down and dirty with him in the best possible way, whenever she felt ready.

Sex helped some people escape, cope temporarily, but it lacked the robust guts of intimacy. Others seemed to retreat into themselves, needing time to think and process at their own pace. Responses, reactions were so individual, as unique as each person on the planet.

Learnings over a lifetime, plus nature and nurture concocted the exclusive mix. He got that, and he imagined she did, too, given her history as a psychologist specializing in trauma. Or she would, once she'd transitioned out of shock.

They stood cradling each other, their chemistry, their energy, potent as all fuck. Undeniable.

He broke away enough to press a tender kiss to her forehead. "Let's wash off the grubbiness of the day and go to bed."

Her smile slayed him with its loving, I-fully-give-myself-to-you, I'm-all-yours intensity.

They showered in caring, affectionate silence, and when they were done, they dried off and curled up in bed, falling asleep within seconds of tangling their limbs together.

* * * *

Chase's ringtone roused Alexander from sleep. With bleary eyes, he patted the bedside table and grabbed his phone.

Eight a.m.

*Fuck.*

He and Sage had gotten to bed less than five hours ago. Alexander wanted to let it go to voicemail, but his conscience wouldn't allow it. He had to make sure his best mate was okay. "Hey, you all right?" he said, his voice low and hoarse.

"So far so good. I'm gonna be a bit black and blue from the crash but, otherwise, I'll make a full recovery. You sound like shit."

"It's been a tough night."

"Is Sage okay?"

"Yeah." *Mostly.*

"Are you?"

"Getting there. And you're calling because...?"

"I wanted to see if you and my sis had hooked up." Alexander could hear the proud, I-got-ya-dude smirk in his voice.

"Right."

"So, you two are together, huh?"

Alexander swallowed. *Here goes...* "Yeah."

"About fucking time."

*"What?"*

"You've had the hots for each other as long as I can remember. You think I didn't notice? No one could miss the attraction...except you two. It was almost comical. Neither of you could push past your bullshit to see the potential."

"So, what are you saying?

"I support your relationship, always have. I'm not one of those overprotective big brothers. I want what's best for my sister, and you're it. I can't imagine any other man suiting her better, any other man I'd trust as much as you."

Relief washed over him like cool, refreshing summer rain. "Thanks. I didn't realize I needed to hear it, but having your blessing makes everything even better."

"So, when's the wedding?"

Alexander chuckled. "Fuck, give me some time! I need to find a ring first."

"No, you don't. She loves you. All she wants is the promise of forever."

One thing he definitely could do. He wouldn't propose anything less.

Sage stirred, turning to snuggle into him, placing her hand on his heart.

Alexander tenderly held his woman to him, careful not to prematurely rouse her from a much-needed rest. "We need to let you know some stuff. If you're free, we'll visit this afternoon."

"Everything all right?"

"It will be."

"O…kay." Chase's voice sounded tentative, wary, concerned.

"Don't stress. We're fine. We'll explain later."

Alexander hung up and his phone rang again. *For fuck's sake.*

"Yeah?

"Alexander Barrett, we need you to come down to the police station to complete your statement." The arresting officer from last night. Did these guys ever sleep? Probably not much when in the midst of a case. He knew all about that. The requirements of the job.

"I'll be there shortly."

"We're trying to get in touch with Sage Cassidy. Do you know how to reach her?"

"I'll bring her with me."

"Great. See you soon."

"Who was that?" Sage trailed her hand over his chest, tracing the lines of his tattoo, her voice barely a whisper, still half asleep.

He ran his palm over her back in soothing, just-chill strokes. "Don't worry."

She searched his eyes. "I am worried."

"No need. When we're ready, we need to get to the police station to give our official statements. And Chase called, too, and he's fine."

Alexander could feel the relieved breath leaving her body. "Thank goodness."

"He supports *us* as well."

"What? Did you tell him?"

"He worked it out."

"Oh. Makes things a lot easier." A massive smile kicked up the corners of her lips. The Sage spell. She'd cast it on him as soon as she'd turned sweet sixteen and, over the years, it had grown more and more powerful.

"Agreed." He cradled her to him. "Not that he had a say."

They kissed, quickly got ready and made it to the precinct in forty-five minutes. The arresting officer joined them and took their individual recounting of events.

Sage tightly clasped Alexander's hand beneath the table, as though to absorb some extra courage. "So, um, do you know if Mallory drove anywhere near the airport the night she kidnapped me?"

The investigator glanced up from his notes and focused his full attention on her. "You're referring to your brother's hit-and-run car accident."

"Yes. It's just, I mean, it was the perfect way to separate me and Alexander."

The guy tapped his pen on the table. "Interesting… We've been looking into that angle as well. Mallory had started working for a security company soon after her husband passed, so had easy access to monitoring and surveillance equipment."

The police officer shifted the paperwork to the side and propped his forearms on the table. "From all the evidence we've gathered, we believe *she* broke into your home and bugged the living area, allowing her to keep track of most of your movements and that of those close to you."

As in him and Chase. Alexander exhaled hard. Fuck. What a fuck up. How had he not thought to check? Why hadn't he instigated a sweep of Sage's house? When he'd worked in the field, he'd have been right on it.

Fucking PTSD, screwing with his head. A floundering fish trying to fit into the flow of civilian life. And being enamored with Sage didn't help, either. Living with the captivating woman had his mind frequently diverting below his belt.

The spyware entirely explained how Mallory had predominantly stayed ahead of them, while devising believable, seemingly faultless excuses.

The policeman flicked his gaze to Alexander, then back to Sage. "Footage we've received places Mallory's car at the scene of the accident, and her phone data usage confirms her trip across town to your office then to her country property."

"And her texts and emails and messages?" Sage firmly clamped her fingers onto the back of Alexander's hand.

A frown furrowed the inspector's face. "We haven't been able to connect those back to her…yet. She may have set up software to prevent IP address location, and used and discarded an additional burner phone."

Alexander leaned in, peering into the officer's eyes. "But you've got enough to get her. She'll go down for this. Yeah?"

"We hope. But she still needs to go to trial, and you'll both have to testify."

No fucking problem — anything they could do to prevent themselves and others from harm. Sometimes the ambiguity with the law really grinded his gears. "Let us know when and where, and we'll be there." Alexander glanced at Sage. "Come on, baby. Let's go home."

# Epilogue

*Six months later*

"When's Chase getting here?" Alexander grabbed Sage's arm as she hurried past and pulled her to him.

"Around seven." She tried to extricate herself. *Yeah, not going to happen.* She pointed to her gold marcasite watch, the one Alexander had given her the day he permanently moved into her place— *their* place— which coincided with their one-month anniversary.

"He's going to arrive any minute!" Her tone said she wanted to finish getting ready, but her eyes clearly expressed she wished he'd treat her to a quickie before her brother invaded their intimate space.

"You've got two choices. One, I go down on you and make you climax in seconds or two, I fuck you against the door and make us both come in less than a minute."

Her breath hitched and she stared into his eyes with a mix of hesitancy and desire.

"Hurry and decide."

Sage Advice

"I want you to come with me."

"I knew you were my soulmate."

She slid out of her lacy scrap of a thong and he pressed her into the closed bedroom door. He bunched up her skirt, and she wrapped her legs around his waist, her arms around his neck.

Alexander ripped open his fly, his erect cock finding her entrance like a heat-seeking missile and drove home, balls deep.

She cried out and urged him on. "Alexander!"

He thrust slow and steady, rubbing his pelvis against her clit. "What do you need, baby?"

"Harder, faster. Get me there! If Chase comes before I get off..."

He didn't even let her finish her sentence, pumping into her with wild, primal abandon. Not even thirty seconds later, she screamed his name.

He chased her orgasm, her insides milking him beautifully and he came, spilling inside her with a force greater than a tsunami.

He smashed his lips to hers in a loving, euphoric kiss, his dick still buried inside her sex.

The doorbell rang.

She held his face. "I told you, he's never late."

"His problem. He can wait." Why did they invite Chase over again?

Oh yeah, because Alexander wanted to test out his new-occupation idea. Get some feedback from those closest to him, those who would affect his choices going forward.

With eyes sparkling, Sage pressed a mind-bending kiss to his lips, and he slipped out of her. "You're fucking hot, baby. Beautiful. I love you so damn much."

"Love you, too." Her smile tracked a path directly to the core of his heart.

"I'll get the door." And he would, except his emotions were still a bit raw. He loved Sage more than life itself and wanted to marry her. But he worried about her opinion on his career decision.

"Okay," she said, and took off into the en suite.

The doorbell rang a second time.

"Coming." He tucked his very satisfied dick into his pants, redid his fly and half-jogged down the stairs to the entrance to let Chase in.

"What was the delay? Or shouldn't I ask?" Her brother's smug smile said he had a pretty good idea about what they'd been doing.

"Don't ask." Alexander waved him in. "Come on through."

He grabbed a beer for himself and his best mate, and a sparkling wine for Sage, then served up their plates of lasagna and Mediterranean salad. Sage soon joined them, and they started eating.

"So, when's the wedding?" Chase said, in between mouthfuls of food.

Sage huff-laughed. "No pressure or anything." She glanced at Alexander.

"Soon. I thought April. You're going to make a beautiful bride." He rubbed his palm along her thigh and squeezed.

She looked almost giddy with elation. "Oh, that's perfect. I *love* April weather!"

"I know."

He couldn't miss the tears of joy glistening in her eyes. And fuck, it almost made him want to take the plunge tomorrow. But the wedding would come around soon enough, assuming she supported his self-funded career prospects. He could be patient. They'd already waited several years, what were a few more months?

She stared at him with an abundance of love and devotion. He fucking wished they were alone so he could show her exactly how much he appreciated her, their relationship.

"Should I go home?" Chase's smirk-filled voice interrupted their little I-love-you-so-much cocoon.

"No." Alexander swung his gaze to his best friend, then back to his woman. "There's something I want to run by you both."

They looked at him with quizzical expressions, ramping up the tension in his body.

Alexander couldn't put the conversation off any longer. He had to explain his intentions, especially before Sage fully committed to him. He didn't want her to feel manipulated or bullied into a situation.

From the moment they'd slept together, literally and figuratively, his nightmares had stopped. He'd kept waiting for them to rear their ugly head but...nothing. *Thank fuck.*

Having her support, and that of the psychologist Sage had arranged, had helped enormously. Now he had to get through this last hurdle.

He had mulled over what it would take to reintegrate into normality, what kind of work would make him happy, fulfilled, feel useful. And he'd chosen a vocation, fear and uncertainty coercing him into holding his controversial cards close to his chest.

"I've decided on something as a possible career."

"You have?" Sage's eyes lit up like a neon sign on the Vegas strip. She'd returned to work after a month's break without any major issues — so far, hopefully never—and had discovered a renewed love of her job. Knowing Mallory had been convicted and put away for several years with regular psychological intervention had also helped.

"Yeah." He inhaled slow and deep. "I want to start a private security company, working on government contracts, as well as weighing up the suitability of any other interesting cases that come along. Before you say anything, let me finish."

They nodded, their gazes steadfast, unblinking.

"I have the experience and the expertise. I won't do many physical assignments—only if the contract calls for it. Mostly, I intend to oversee operations and employ ex-military, ex-police force, ex-firefighters, anyone who still has the drive to protect others but can't return to their previous occupation. I want to hire those who have the skills and desire to re-find purpose in their lives."

He chanced a glance at Chase first, then Sage. Their beaming smiles reinforced their support and unconditional love. "I was thinking of calling it 'Solve Security'. Solve cases, solve ex-service people's concerns and uncertainty about new career options, about where they fit in. What do you think?"

"It's fucking fantastic—the idea, the name." Chase slapped him hard on the shoulder and grinned.

Alexander grinned back. One down, one to go. He swept his gaze to his woman and waited for her response. His heart hadn't pounded this hard since he worried he might lose the love of his life.

She smiled, big and broad and full-on affectionate. "I think it's brilliant. And we'll assist you in any way we can to get the project up and going."

Thank fuck he had plenty of capital from good investments as well as his military payout and pension. Plus the closest, most important people understood his need to engage in meaningful activity or else he'd struggle.

He blew out a relieved breath. "Thank you. You don't know how much this whole venture hinged on your backing—not that I'd planned to put pressure on either of you or anything."

They both laughed.

Sage climbed onto Alexander's lap, giving him an amazing squish hug. Protecting his woman, helping save her life, saved his. Her love for him provided the priceless added bonus.

No, more than that. It sustained him, added to his resolve, solidified a new strong foundation.

He had dropped his vocational bombshell on them, and they'd responded even better than he'd hoped. He really had surrounded himself with the best possible people—kind, loving, compassionate, understanding. They had his back, and he had theirs...now and forever.

Alexander delved into the front pocket of his jeans and met Sage's gaze. "I suppose I should make it all official, you know, confirm you want to marry me?"

"Of course I do! April bride, remember?"

A full-on ecstatic smile stretched almost to the edges of his face.

"Now, where's my ring?" She grabbed his closed hand and tried to pry it open.

He and Chase chuckled. *So Sage.*

Alexander unfurled his fingers, exposing the piece of expensive vintage jewelry, sitting atop his palm.

She gasped.

Just the response he'd hoped for because, yeah, he'd bought the exact type of design she'd dreamed about as a teenager.

The moment he'd decided to propose, he'd selected the 'Sage engagement ring' file from his brain—a solitaire canary diamond—and searched for it. Going by her reaction, he'd found the perfect replica.

"How did you...? You noticed." She said it like she couldn't quite believe he got her so well...even now.

Tears spilled onto her cheeks, and he swiped away the descending drops with the pad of his thumb. "I always took notice of you, and I always will."

"Awww... You two are sickeningly sweet. Fucking fructose to the max. If dinner wasn't five-star Michelin standard, I'd be regurgitating it right now." Chase stared at them with a pleased, I-knew-it, I'm-giving-you-shit-cause-I-can expression.

Alexander held his future wife against him and stared at his brother-in-law-to-be. "Well, you better get your responses under control because you're going to be my best man."

Chase raised his glass and saluted them. "Best night *ever*!"

Sage kissed her brother on the cheek then Alexander on the lips. "Couldn't have said it more eloquently myself."

Alexander couldn't agree more.

# Want to see more from this author? Here's a taster for you to enjoy!

# Oh, Baby: The Best-Laid Plans
## Sandra Carmel

### *Excerpt*

"What do you mean? This is bullshit!" Archer Aldrich stomped across the expansive floor of his plush office and stared through the window at the gridlocked traffic below — the new norm in Melbourne's central business district.

His great-uncle Salvator had died in 2011. *Fucking twelve years ago.* And until Archer's grandma passed away recently, he'd had no idea about the guy's will. Fuck, he hadn't even been eligible to inherit until now. Apparently those before him had failed to meet the stipulations, and he was the next — and last — in line.

"Maybe, but legally, I can't do anything about it. The only way for you to receive your full entitlement is to find a wife…and the sooner, the financially more viable. The conditions state you need to marry before Valentine's Day."

What the fuck? How could his solicitor sound so matter-of-fact, so calm? How could he not think the whole thing was irrational? Ludicrous. Overly sickly saccharine. A total dreamer's mentality. The fucking stats, the data, showed that one in two marriages ended in divorce.

So if not for some stupid will proviso, what drove people down the committed monogamy path? Why bother searching for a supposedly special needle in a stack of similar needles?

Made absolutely no sense. There were so many attractive, available women. Why settle for only one? "Come on. There has to be some way to break such a ridiculous, outdated requirement."

"Unfortunately not. Believe me, I've investigated all options, and I can't supersede the soulmate clause."

Archer massaged his forehead with firm, inflexible fingers. What was with his great-uncle? The guy had become so obsessed with soulmates he'd even developed a serum to determine whether someone was a person's fated life partner. Could he *really* be related to Salvator? Their beliefs were practically polar opposites.

Who fucking cared about finding 'the one'? Why not enjoy every individual partner for their contribution to each unique experience. "So...what? I need to find a woman I like and marry her before the fourteenth of February? That's only a few months away." He huffed. "And if I don't?"

"You receive a small consolatory amount, and the bulk of the money goes to the Jade and Violet Vampire Foundation to support health and wellbeing in the vampire community."

Archer swore under his breath, frustrated as all fuck. "You have to be kidding me. Salvator didn't even have any vampire genetics!"

"Would I joke about something like this?"

No, the guy wouldn't. He had nothing to gain. But Archer did. A whole fucking huge stash of cash. The way Salvator had invested, it would set him up for the rest of his life. Hell, extend way beyond it.

He'd be a total fuckhead if he looked this unconventional gift horse in the mouth. "Fine. You'll be the first to hear about my engagement." Archer stabbed his index finger at the red 'end call' button, and threw his phone onto the desk.

Fuck, he didn't even have a love interest, a regular date. Didn't even believe in the institution of marriage. And the festive season had already started with no female prospects.

The countdown to Christmas had commenced, leaving just a measly few months to not only find an agreeable woman but also convince her to marry him.

*No pressure. Yeah.* He dropped into his office chair, his head in his hands. Like he fucking needed this extra stress… Like it wasn't already a massive pain in the ass ensuring his company made a profit while ignoring the unexplainable attraction he had to his Norwegian business partner's sexy sister…

Not conventionally sexy. Sort of sexy in a nerdy way. Not normally his type, but something about her got him going. Probably her hybrid vampire genetics. Probably the forbidden aspect. Probably the fact that he couldn't have her, even though every one of her actions screamed for a Dominant's direction. *His* direction.

Archer normally couldn't resist a challenge, but in this instance, he had to. He couldn't hook up with his friend's sweet sister unless he aimed for more of a future. He couldn't screw her over — not that he'd plan to, but shit happened — or his business partner buddy, to satisfy a short-term need.

His cock disagreed, desperate to sink into her wet heat. But he couldn't take advantage. *No fucking way.* That would break the 'bro' business code, as well as his strong scrupulous stance.

He might have a history of changing women more often than he changed his underwear, but every relationship he entered into was one hundred percent consensual. No matter what people believed, he did have an honorable bone in his body.

Did he struggle to accept the restrictive circumstances? Ignore his Neanderthal needs? Fuck, yes. Ever since Temperance Elskelig had arrived in Melbourne on a working visa, he'd had an extremely hard time resisting the woman.

But he refused to cross the lustful line, despite how often his sinful side begged him to have her just once. If he did give in to his impulses, his whole life could come crashing down around him like persistent, pelting rockfall, burying him under an avalanche of regret. The roll-on effect destroying her, too.

Wrong.

So fucking wrong and supremely selfish.

Although he wanted her on a primal level, acknowledged it, he couldn't lead her on or pretend he could offer her forever, when he had never even shown a propensity for staying the night after a hookup. Had never had a long-term relationship...unless a couple of weeks met the criteria.

Yeah...no.

A knock sounded on his office door. "Archer? Are you available?"

Not usually, but for Temperance, the woman in question...? Her sweet, melodic voice penetrated the timber and touched a spot deep within him, right in the vicinity of his usually impenetrable heart.

His principles ensured his conquests clearly understood his intentions, but until her, no one had ever broken the lust barrier.

Did she have ESP? Had she tuned in to his complicated thoughts? Everyone knew that those with vampire genetics often had special powers.

"Come in." If only he could.

*Enough.*

Time to dial back the debauchery and switch into professional boss mode.

Temperance eased the door open and stepped inside, a nervous smile tugging at the corners of her luscious lips. She avoided eye contact, as usual, her long, wavy bronze hair framing her beautiful face.

If she didn't know it already, she qualified as the quintessential submissive, another endearing trait he couldn't ignore. It spoke right to his inner Dom.

His cock agreed, saluting her stunning presence. And thankfully, although painfully, it remained confined in his suddenly too-tight pants. Having her so close, in his space, his lust-o-meter practically redlined. He wanted to forget protocol, forget sensibility, stride over to the temptress and slam his mouth onto hers.

He'd lost count of how many times he'd masturbated before bed, imagining her bound and gagged and on display for his pleasure...and hers, because a huge part of him getting off relied on pleasing his partner. No, not purely pleasing — taking her right to the outer extremes of ecstasy.

"Sir, I have the reports you requested." Her use of *Sir*, combined with her Scandinavian accent sent a surge of desire directly to his dick. She stumbled across the room and deposited said reports on his desk. Averted eyes, shaky hands, soft voice. Sexy as fuck.

*Sir*. How he wanted her to address him in that way outside of work. In the back of his car, on his couch, on his kitchen bench, in his bedroom, in the spa — over and over and over.

*Stop it.*

He had to rein in his thinking before he lost all sense of decorum and acted on his overpowering urges. "You could have emailed them." His voice came out choppy, abrupt, strangled.

"I've done that, too. With your meeting this afternoon, I thought you might want a hard copy to review prior, to make notes on and highlight any relevant sections."

How could someone be so fucking smart, innocent and sexy all in one irresistible package? He forced himself to stay behind his desk and gripped tight to the last vestiges of his usually ironclad control. "Thank you."

She glanced at him — the first time their eyes had met since she'd entered the room and, fuck, did they pack a powerful punch — her forehead furrowed as though shocked. Had he gone too hardass, alpha boss-hole in the past, in an attempt to keep her beyond arm's length? Been too gruff, brash, hardcore Dom?

*Shit, yeah.* He'd done whatever he could so she, and her brother, had not even the tiniest hint of his attraction to her.

She shifted from foot to foot and studied her now-empty hands as though they were the most interesting things she'd ever observed. "Um, do you need anything else?"

Aside from her straddling his lap and him kissing her senseless? Driving his dick deep between her gorgeous legs and fucking her until she screamed his name?

"Not at the moment. Thanks." His curt, dismissive 'me-master, you-servant' tone had her racing to exit his office like she couldn't wait to escape.

Had he scared her? Been too intimidating? *Most likely.* People had given him that feedback many times over the years, plus added a few other choice words. But he didn't want her to think of him as aloof or arrogant, or to instill fear in the sweet little sub. He craved her respect. A massive difference.

Archer pushed out of his office chair, headed to the coffee-pod machine in his mini bar and took his freshly made macchiato to the window. Cars still sat bumper-to-bumper, but some movement had returned.

*What a fucking day.* First the weird-ass will criteria, then the Temperance temptation. He needed to stop fixating on her and her unavailability and focus on finding a fake wife—at least until he met the full terms of his inheritance. Someone he liked who'd agree to a short-term, paid arrangement, preferably with perks.

Yeah, okay, it sounded crass and cheap, but not with the right person. Ideally he'd choose someone who, like him, had their own agenda, which included having fun as part of the deal.

But who in his regular social circle met that criterion? He had a sip of his coffee. *Rich, full-bodied, aromatic. Fucking perfect.* His mind searched through candidates...

It had to be someone who wouldn't want more. Would accept the need-to-be-wed-by-Valentine's-Day terms, preferably stay married for at least a few weeks and play along, knowing he'd remunerate them. The woman would receive a healthy sum of money to successfully set up her own life. He wouldn't offer anything less.

She'd be handsomely compensated for a scant few months of her time. He sifted through his back catalog of feasible female contacts. Who could he trust to not only agree to the terms but also ensure the curious cat didn't flee from the flimsy bag?

An extensive history of women paraded through his head. *No, no, no, no, no.* He grabbed his mobile phone off the desk and scrolled through his long list of friends-with-benefits. Maybe he'd missed someone?

Nope.

Archer couldn't imagine spending longer than a few nights in one hit, let alone several months with any of them. Hence why they'd been relegated to past flings or occasional hook-ups, and he was still single.

Man, he was fucked. So fucked. Not one woman stood out in his mind, except the one he couldn't have.

Temperance.

Normally he loved the chance to overcome adversity, loved to tackle and conquer whatever he, or others, believed he couldn't do. It developed strength of character and positive forward movement.

However, the Temperance situation was a fuck-ton more complicated.

He blew out a frustrated breath, dropped his phone back on the desk and ran his fingers through his hair.

His mobile buzzed, his business partner's face filling the screen. Bror, Temperance's brother. What fucked-up timing? Had the guy sensed something? Was he another hybrid with special powers? One way to find out for sure.

He answered the video call on the fourth ring. "Hey, mate, what can I do you for?"

"I have a favor to ask." The guy had an unblinking stare that would scare the fuck out of most people, but not Archer. He'd known Bror for years. They'd met at a business conference in America and had kept in touch, their close friendship morphing into a collective enterprise.

It hadn't taken long for Archer to determine the difference between when the guy wanted to discuss something serious or was truly pissed off.

"Go ahead." Hopefully he'd read him accurately and the guy's request wouldn't make his day any more difficult.

"Temperance needs a husband."

*What?* And he was asking him because? "Why?" Archer focused on keeping his expression curious yet neutral.

"To get fast-tracked approval for a permanent visa. Do you know someone…suitable?"

What the fuck did *suitable* mean? A good guy, a hybrid, a full Jade or Violet? Didn't make a difference. Not to him. "No." No fucking way. He wouldn't let any of the single guys he knew touch her, whether they had vampire genetics or not. He couldn't stand any other male pawing her, full fucking stop.

"Are you sure?"

He stared at his mate's practically pleading face on his mobile phone screen, not quite believing what he'd heard. "Does she know you're doing this?"

"Not exactly. She has repeatedly said how much she's enjoyed her stay, and it would be great for business having a reliable vampire community rep in Australia. She already has several contacts and could make more.

"Unfortunately, given my input in the business, we can't sponsor her. So in order to get her visa approved ASAP, she needs to get married. Then, if the guy doesn't work out, she can find a more appropriate, longer-term husband."

So, anyone half-decent would do for the interim as long as they helped her get permanent residency, but for a serious relationship, did the guy need to have vampire genetics? Did her brother's assessment of what sort of man constituted marriage material reflect her thoughts and beliefs, too?

Would she not consider a full-human guy, if she found him attractive and they connected mentally and emotionally, as well as on a practical level? Would the cultural differences be too much of a deterrent?

"Even though you don't currently know anyone, now that you're aware of the situation and the broad-reaching positive ramifications for all of us, I'd really appreciate it if you'd keep your eyes peeled for possibilities."

This guy was un-fucking-believable. Yeah, he may have a point about it benefiting their business, but he was playing his sister like a pawn. Fuck that. No way could he betray her, put her in a compromising position, unless she understood the full terms and consented.

Hang on... Why get so worked up? It didn't matter who she chose as a long-term partner. Maybe he could help her in the short term. The perfect guy, and all his positive attributes, appeared in his brain.

Someone who didn't want forever but would treat her right. Fill her in on any important details, provide respect, and factor in her opinions, keep her abreast of decisions. Make the whole experience fucking unforgettable. Make it mutually satisfying.

"Sure." Maybe the universe had heard his pleas...

# About the Author

Sandra Carmel is an Australian author of racy, flirty and downright-dirty romance novels, novellas, short stories and poetry, who enjoys stimulating herself and others with words. An obsession with classic romance novels, particularly Jane Eyre, and her infatuation with Mr Rochester were key motivators in commencing her romance writing journey. So far, she has taken the scenic route from steamy paranormal to sci-fi to contemporary, creating provocative stories that delve beneath the surface of desire. She reads and writes a lot, frequently disrupted by her ever-attentive, cheeky cats, and sinfully amorous array of book boyfriends.

Sandra loves to hear from readers. You can find her contact information, website details and author profile page at https://www.totallybound.com

Home of Erotic Romance

Sign up for our newsletter and find out about all our romance book releases, eBook sales and promotions, sneak peeks and FREE romance books!

www.ingramcontent.com/pod-product-compliance
Lightning Source LLC
Chambersburg PA
CBHW020618250626
47154CB00004B/1567